INK

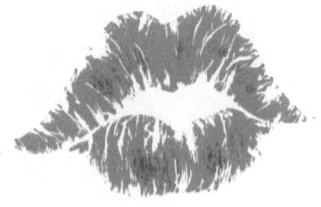

EVERNIGHT PUBLISHING ®

www.evernightpublishing.com

SAM CRESCENT

Copyright© 2023 Sam Crescent

ISBN: 978-0-3695-0813-3

Cover Artist: Sour Cherry Designs

Jacket Design: Jay Aheer

Editor: Karyn White

INK

DEDICATION

Thank you so much to all my Skulls and Chaos Bleeds fans. You're all amazing and so supportive.

INK

The Skulls, 17

Sam Crescent

Copyright © 2019

Chapter One

Cancer.

Acute Lymphoblastic Leukemia.

ALL for short.

Darcy stared out of the hospital room's window, watching as her parents listened to the good doctor on the best course of treatment. There was no time for waiting around. If they waited too long, there was a higher chance she would die. Not that there was any less of a chance. It seemed almost surreal. Like it wasn't happening to her.

Biting her lip, she climbed off the bed, and Ink stood up. Yeah, she had to have a Skull in her hospital room at all times. She just wanted some fresh air. No matter how much her body ached, she just wanted to be outside, to be away from all of this.

This wasn't fair.

Not even a little bit.

Especially as the Skull who was with her was

none other than Ink, the very guy she'd had a crush on for some time. It was hard to be around him. She tried to avoid him at all costs, apart from when she could watch him without getting caught. She liked doing that. He always had his shirt off, and she got to see his heavily inked chest, and it certainly was a sight to behold, one she particularly loved to see.

"I'm fine," she said. She didn't want him to see her as weak or ill.

"You really should relax."

"Really? I'm fine." She was sick and tired of everyone telling her to relax, that everything was fine. If she was fucking *fine* then she wouldn't be in the hospital and her mother wouldn't be crying her eyes out as her father held her.

This wasn't fine, not even close.

Ink shouldn't be here. There were so many Skulls. Why did her dad have to pick him? It's not like he knew she had this giant crush on Ink, and if he did, it sucked he'd even allow him to be near her.

Not that she minded.

Most days when Ink took care of her, she didn't mind, but this was different. Her hair was a mess. She felt sick to her stomach, and the last time she looked in the mirror, a ghost was staring right back at her.

"You're not fine, Darcy, and you know it," Ink said. He held her elbow in his hand, and it irritated her that he'd do this now. She would have remembered every single time he touched her, but instead, it had to be now, while she was in the hospital, sick and not just any sickness either.

The C-word.

The dreaded word that always caused the smile from people's faces to drop. This was her. She'd suck the energy and the love out of the room.

"I don't want to get back into bed," she said. Tears were so close, but she held them at bay. There's no way she'd allow him to see her cry. The pity in his gaze was too much.

"You need to rest and relax, and let us all take care of you."

She shook her head.

"Come on, Darcy. Don't do this."

"I don't want to be sick," she said. "I'm not sick. I feel fine. They've got those stupid tests all mixed up and wrong. It happens all the time. Someone makes a mistake, and that's what has happened with me. They made a mistake." Even as she said the words, she knew it was all lies.

The tiredness, the achiness. A small bump and she bruised so easily.

It was all part of it, and she hated it, hated it all. Knowing the doctors were right.

Ink didn't let go of her arm even as she wanted to collapse on the floor.

She pressed her hands to her face and took several deep breaths. She felt like she was drowning. Everyone was constantly giving percentages and statistics, as if that would help. She didn't need numbers flashed before her.

This wasn't some math equation she had to work out. This was real life, her life.

She was sick, and even though the percentage of survival and full cure were high for her age group, fifteen, there was still a small chance she may not make it.

Dead at a young age.

Being one of The Skulls' members' daughters, Darcy had grown up around death. She'd heard how people talked about death and how some died way too young. What about her? She was young, so young.

She'd never left Fort Wills for longer than to go and see the Chaos Bleeds crew. Her entire life had been about growing up, school, being part of the club.

At fifteen she'd never even been kissed.

She could die a virgin.

Die without ever telling Ink how she felt, or being old enough for him to consider her feelings for him as more than a stupid crush.

Pulling out of his hold, she gave him her back, gripping the edge of the bed.

"Darcy?"

"You don't have to stay here. I'm fine. I can deal with this myself." She just couldn't handle Ink being this close, especially now.

Even though she wanted him out of her room, he still helped her back into the bed.

"You need to keep your strength up and be ready to fight. Remember that. You're a fucking fighter. You don't quit."

"Are you done?" she asked, settling against the cushions, hating herself for how petulant she was being.

This was unfair. She hated it. Hated everything.

"Look at me, Darcy. You're going to beat this. You hear me? You're going to beat this."

The tears wouldn't stop. They wouldn't back down, and she felt sick to her stomach.

"Really? You're going to be the one to guarantee it? Not even a doctor would do that." She shook her head. "Please, just leave me alone."

Ink hesitated for a split second, but he stepped away from her bed. She turned her head, looking toward the window. The sun was shining through, and more than anything, she wished she was outside. Ink didn't leave though. Out of the corner of her eye, she saw him still sitting, watching her. Every now and then he'd grab his cell phone and click away at the screen, but he didn't pay her any attention.

She knew he was taking care of her though.

He wouldn't allow anything bad to happen to her. She knew from her years of being with The Skulls, it wouldn't happen.

Lying back on the bed, she closed her eyes, wishing for something, anything to happen. Staying in bed all day was starting to wear on her last nerve.

"You know you're a strong girl, Darcy."

She squeezed her eyes closed, wishing he wasn't talking even as his voice made her feel so many different things.

"I don't want to talk about this right now."

"It's not going to change the fact you've got cancer. The doctor will come up with a treatment plan. You'll get better."

She sat up in bed, glaring at him. "How can you be so sure about something like this? It's cancer, Ink. It's not the flu or a bad case of the sniffles."

"The survival rate is impeccable."

"But there's still a chance I could die," she said. "No one seems to grasp that."

"Are you just going to give up? You're not going to fight?"

"It wouldn't be giving up if I just didn't take treatment. I could live my life. Make some new experiences."

"You're fifteen years old, Darcy. There's no chance of that ever happening."

She swiped at the tears that fell down her face, angry she was even allowing this to get to her. This was her life as well, and no matter what they fucking did, she wasn't going to allow anyone to tell her what to do. "I can do whatever the hell I want."

"Yeah, then try doing that without passing out. You're exhausted. You're ill If you don't go for treatment, you're going to die. Stop being so fucking stubborn about this, and be the fighter Blaine and Emily raised. You're not a quitter. Stop behaving like one."

The door opened as Blaine and Emily entered. Her parents. They were both pale, but she saw the hope in their eyes. They believed there would be a happily ever after. She didn't believe in fairy tales.

"So, we've spoken with the doctor, and we're in agreement. You're to start treatment right away," Blaine said.

"I'm going to stay with you," Emily said. "Blaine's going to grab you some stuff, and well, you're always going to have company. You're not going to be alone."

She looked at her parents, and she knew without a doubt, no matter what she said, they were going to overrule her.

Glancing between them, she noticed Ink watching her, and he smirked.

No matter what she wanted, she was going to have to have the treatment. She was so scared of screwing up.

"Okay, so what's first?"
****

Ink walked into The Skulls' clubhouse and went right up to the bar, grabbing a bottle of scotch. He didn't even bother with a glass.

"Bad day?" Steven asked.

"You know I was on Darcy duty, right?"

Steven winced, slapping him on the back. "It'll be fine."

He burst out laughing. "It'll be fine?"

"You've got to think positively about this."

"There's nothing to think or to feel, for fuck's sake. There's a fifteen-year-old girl about to undergo treatment for cancer. There's no way this can go any better?"

"At least she's in a good place."

Ignoring his friend, he downed a couple of glugs of strong scotch, relishing the instant burn as it traveled down his throat. That was the stuff. He needed to do something so he stopped thinking about that young woman sitting on the hospital bed, fucking scared for her life. She was only a child. A teenager.

There was no way in fucking hell she should be going through this shit.

He glanced around the clubhouse, hoping to find a slut to take his mind off the troubling thoughts.

Nothing. None of the women appealed to him.

"You're angry."

"No shit." He ran a hand down his face in an attempt to clear the fog from his mind. He was really struggling with everything right now. Darcy was a sweet person.

"Does this have to do with the fact Darcy has a crush?"

Ink glared at Steven, not interested in the slightest to have this kind of conversation. They all knew about Steven's relationship with Sally. Sally was Whizz and Lacey's adopted teenage daughter, who had developed a crush on Steven. That crush had nearly sent Sally into the arms of another man until Steven realized he wanted her just as much as she wanted him.

This wasn't like that. Darcy was a teenager. A sick one.

"Don't, man."

"What? Darcy is not going to stay young forever.

You've got to see that."

He wanted Darcy to grow up because she had a right to grow up, not for anything else.

"I'm done with this shit." He grabbed his bottle and headed out, avoiding the small play area. He didn't want to see any kids playing or be responsible for anything.

Finding a nice, quiet area to sit and just enjoy his drink, he sat down on the hard ground, leaning against the brickwork.

Pulling out his pack of smokes, he knew he needed to quit, but he'd only used them as a treat for himself. Lighting up, he took a long drag on the nicotine before blowing it out into a cloud in front of his face. Next, he took a swig of his drink.

Nothing could get better than this.

"You're going to drink yourself to passing out?" Lash asked.

Ink groaned. "Are you going to tell me you want me for something?"

"Don't I always?"

"Please, can I just have this afternoon where I pretend to be a lowlife drunk?" Ink asked, looking at his Prez.

"You can do whatever you want." Lash lowered himself to the ground with a groan. "You don't want to be around the kids?"

"I don't think the kids should be around me while I'm, you know, not the best company." He took another swig, and feeling guilty, he quickly offered some up for Lash to take.

Lash chuckled, taking a sip.

"Will Angel be pissed at you?"

"Angel doesn't have a pissed bone in her body. It'll be fine. She's worried, anyway."

Ink stared down at the ground. "She's too young."

"Angel?"

"No, Darcy. Why would Angel be too young?"

"No reason." Lash chuckled. "I guess I'm used to people telling me my relationship with Angel was doomed to fail."

"No, it wasn't. You guys are … everything."

"You're starting to sound a little romantic there, Ink."

"No romantic. If there were two people meant for each other, it was you and Angel. It's plain fucking logic. Tate and Murphy as well, but mostly you and Angel."

"Are you okay?" Lash asked.

"I'll be fine. Are you doing the whole babysitting routine here, *Prez*?"

Lash sighed. "Darcy is just a kid, you know. She's smart, funny, and way too young to have to be going through this. I got to make sure my guys are ready. The Billionaire pussies will call when they need us, and we can't all stick around with Darcy."

"You're going to make sure she's protected though, right?"

"Of course. Darcy will always have someone with her. I know the hospital's policy, but a nice healthy donation and they turn a blind eye to someone always with her. She will get the protection she needs." Lash handed him back the bottle. "I can't imagine what Emily and Blaine are going through right now."

Ink nodded.

"You know Darcy's got a huge crush on you. When you babysit her or spend time with her, try not to look so perfect," Lash said in between chuckles.

"What the fuck does that mean?"

"It means protect the young girl's heart. She will

go fucking crazy for you."

"Ah," Angel said, rounding the corner of the building. She walked toward them and Lash got to his feet, pulling his woman into his arms.

Ink watched them. He saw the blush on Angel's cheeks. No matter how many times Lash touched her, held her, or kissed her, she never lost that stroke of innocence that always seemed to cling to her.

"I thought I'd find you here. Steven said you'd gone looking for Ink." She turned to him. "How is she?"

"Angry. When I was with her, she wanted to avoid treatment."

Angel gasped. "She did?"

"Yep. It won't happen though. She's a minor. Her parents control her course of medication." Ink took a long drink of his scotch, noticing how Lash held his wife, the natural way they touched each other. No one was interfering with them. Their love over the years had grown stronger, and Ink had never made a comment about them before. He'd watched their relationship, and as he was getting older, he knew, deep down, he wanted something like that.

"The school has already set her work. She'll be staying in the hospital during the course of treatment," Lash said. "She'll keep up to date with her studies. It'll keep her mind occupied. Michael will take her classwork to her after school."

Michael was Alex's son from a previous hookup, but that was a longer story, and Ink didn't want to think about Butch.

"Are you needing me to pick Michael up?" he asked.

"You've already drunk a quarter bottle of scotch," Lash said. "Your ass is grounded for the night."

"Okay, Dad, you won't take my pocket money

from me next, will you?"

"Asshole," Lash said.

Angel laughed. "He does act like a dad a lot, doesn't he?"

"I doubt he plays something like that with you," Ink said.

If it was possible, Angel's face got even redder.

"We've got work do to," Lash said. "Don't do anything stupid, and give me your keys."

"I won't ride."

"I don't give a fuck. You know my rules, and you'll abide by them."

Ink groaned as he reached into his pocket, pulling out the keys Lash wanted. When he slapped them into Lash's hand, his Prez nodded at him, and they both turned to leave. Ink stayed where he was, with his scotch and cigarettes.

He heard the kids laughing in the distance, and he rested his head back against the wall. His temples were throbbing, and he knew it was because of the stress.

He loved The Skulls so damn much. They were all a family, and he'd prospected here for a long time before finally getting his leather cut and patch. When he did, he'd been so damn proud, so happy. Never had he belonged to anything quite so powerful, at least not to him. He didn't mind the shit they had to go through. The battles, the fear, the risks. He'd die for each and every single member of the club, and he'd do it with a smile on his face, especially if he knew it would protect them.

They were his only family.

Time ticked by and he heard the call for food, but he didn't get up. The sun began to set, and he opened his eyes as darkness slowly descended.

Movement to his left drew his attention, and he saw Michael, the little shit that was Alex's kid, with some weed.

"What the fuck are you doing?" he asked, startling the kid.

Since they'd struck a deal with the law and were now helping the Billionaires, their old life had taken a dramatic turn. No drugs, no guns, no illegal shit.

They were all legit, and it was because of Lash that it was the case.

No one had any complaints about it, seeing as all the crap they had to deal with leading up to their going legit.

"Put that fucking out now before I get your dad on your ass. You want to play the big tough kid, you'll do it inside a cell."

"You wouldn't," Michael shot back.

"I would, and with you, I wouldn't even give a fuck."

Chapter Two

Darcy put the book down. She'd done as much homework as she could stand right now. The sounds of the hospital were all around her. Steven was now on babysitting duty, but he'd gone to grab himself a coffee.

Tucking her hair behind her ear, she wondered if she'd be one of the people who ended up losing her hair. There were so many different side effects and scary possibilities. The doctor had gone through them all, but she hadn't heard them, not after he said the whole cancer thing, and what she was going to have to do.

"You shouldn't be alone," Sandy said, entering her room.

Sandy was Stink's old lady, a doctor, and a part of The Skulls.

"Hey," she said.

Sandy leaned against the bed and grabbed her chart. "How are you doing today?"

"Are you being my doctor?"

"Sorry, I can't seem to shut it off."

Darcy smiled.

Sandy was the only one not treating her as sick. After she glanced through the chart then put it back in place, she picked up one of the assignment sheets she was sent. "It's the only part that sucks, you still have to do homework. They won't give you a reprieve."

"You're not a cancer doctor, are you?"

"No, I'm not. I wouldn't be able to be on your case anyway. Not with something like this. I thought Steven was supposed to be keeping you company."

"He got thirsty and went for coffee. I'm fine. I was doing homework and reading."

Sandy reached out, taking hold of her hand. "You're being very brave."

"You're not going to give me pity as well, are you?"

"Why would I give you pity?" Sandy asked.

"I don't know. Everyone is treating me with kid gloves."

"And you're finding it hard to settle on one emotion. You're sad, then angry, and then you hate everyone and everything."

"How do you know that?"

"I know you, and I know patients."

"I don't want to be a patient."

"I know that also. This is one of the scariest moments you're ever going to have." Sandy took hold of her hand. "But you are strong. You can do this."

"You're not going to tell me to beat it."

"You know you've got to beat it, otherwise you won't get a chance to chase after Ink when you're all better."

"Oh, please, I don't know what the big deal is. I'm not with him. I'm not even close to him. We are nothing to each other."

Sandy chuckled. "So say all the women who don't want the guy to know."

"It doesn't matter."

"Am I interrupting?"

Darcy looked toward the door to see Tabitha.

"Not at all, darling. You come and keep our girl company. I'm going to have a word with Steven." Sandy was gone before Darcy could say anything.

"Oops, he's in trouble, isn't he?" Tabitha asked, walking into the room.

"What are you doing here?"

"I walked here."

"You cut school?"

"It's not like it's hard to do." Tabitha dragged the

chair across the room.

Darcy knew when Tabitha was a few years older, she was going to drive people crazy. She was a law unto herself, and Eva and Tiny thought they could confine that attitude, but there was no controlling Tabitha. She was so independent, always had been, even at a young age.

"You know, I used to hate coming to the hospital, but I think I could get used to this." Tabitha sat down, her hands resting across her stomach as she smiled over at Darcy.

"You really should be in school."

"School is lame. At least it is right now. I miss you. It sucks without you."

Darcy sighed, lifting up her books. "I'm still doing work."

"Michael bring you that stuff?"

"Yep."

"I'd check everything in case he uses you to do his homework."

Darcy rolled her eyes. "He still trying to do that shit?"

"I know he doesn't like school, and he keeps trying to get other girls to do his homework for him. I'm going to have to cut him."

"Tabitha?"

"What? He's a grade-A asshole. No one wants to admit it, but it is the truth. He needs to be taught a lesson."

"Cut him?"

"I have a knife."

"How did you get a knife?" Tabitha stayed quiet. "I'm not joking around. A knife is really dangerous, and Michael is an *asshole*, we all know that. If he overpowers you, what are you going to do?"

"I'm young, but I'm not stupid. I can hurt him."

She shrugged. "Simon gave it to me."

"Simon gave you the knife."

"Bingo. He wanted me to have it to protect myself. He hates being away from me." Tabitha sighed. "I hate being away from him too. I miss him so much."

Darcy stared at her friend. They weren't the same age. Darcy was a couple of years older than Tabitha, but they connected. They both had a love of their family and the club, and because of that love, they'd grown close really quickly. Also, they had grown up together.

What if she never saw Tabitha and Simon's wedding? What if she … was dead? She'd never be able to watch her family grow up, and she'd just be dead.

"Don't do Michael's homework for him," Tabitha said, pulling Darcy out of her thoughts.

She didn't like how dark her thoughts went. Lifting up her blanket, she showed Tabitha the homework that Michael had tried to sneak in to get her to do. "I'm sick, but I can still see when Michael is trying to take the piss."

"I think he needs to go back to Vegas."

Darcy laughed. "Alex will deal with him."

"Really? Uncle Alex doesn't seem to have a handle on him. No one does."

"And you think you can put him in his place?"

"Hell, yeah. He doesn't scare me. He never has."

"Just be careful, okay? I don't like the thought of him hurting you."

"Please, he can't hurt anyone. It's Michael. I'll kick his ass, or I'll get Miles and Anthony to do it."

Darcy paused. Miles, Anthony, and Tabitha were all the same age, but they were deadly, including Daisy. They were a foursome at school. The Skulls often stuck together, but Michael wasn't playing by the rules.

"Okay," Darcy said.

"You like the idea of Michael getting his ass kicked, don't you?" Tabitha asked, laughing.

"It would be funny." She didn't like Michael. His time in Vegas had made him mean and spiteful. "Let's talk about something else."

"I heard Ink was here the other day."

"What is it with everyone talking about Ink?" Darcy asked, sitting back. "Nothing is going to happen, and I don't even have a crush on him anymore."

"You don't?" Tabitha asked, brow raised.

"Stop looking at me like that."

"Like what?"

"Like I'm lying to you."

"I know you're lying to me. I'm not judging you for it. I believe Sally was the same."

"It's not the same."

"Why not?"

"Because, Sally was closer to Steven's age, and well, I'm not."

"So, you won't be a teenager forever."

"You do know you're younger than me."

"It doesn't mean I don't know things." She shrugged. "Look at my mom and dad. They have a huge age gap. He's, like, granddaddy age, but they love each other. I've never seen my mom look at anyone else the way she does my dad. Why can't it work with you and Ink?"

Darcy stared at Tabitha. There was no fighting with this girl; she seemed to have an argument for everything.

"You snuck out of school again?" Steven asked, entering the room with a coffee in hand.

"You know me."

"I do, and I know your dad is going to be pissed."

Tabitha shrugged. "It'll be fine. He knows I'm

here for Darcy and nothing more."

Darcy smiled.

"How are you feeling?" Steven asked.

For a few minutes, Darcy was able to forget she was a sick person and what that kind of sickness meant. She tried not to think about what was to come. The medication, the treatment, the side effects.

Staring at Tabitha, she wished she was like her friend. Confident, happy, healthy, so sure of herself, and not once would she allow anyone to put her down.

"Of course she's feeling fine. Look at her, she's awesome and is in total control, isn't that right?" Tabitha said.

"Yes, total control."

It was all lies, though. She didn't feel in control, far from it.

Tabitha and Steven began to talk, and she looked down at her lap, at the schoolwork stretched out before her. She couldn't help but wonder what Ink was doing right at that very moment.

****

Ink rubbed at his head as he walked down the main clubhouse stairs to the kitchen. The scent of food was making him feel sick, but if food was being made, it meant Angel was in the kitchen, and if she was in the kitchen, that meant he was going to get coffee, which was what he needed.

Everyone had their own hangover cure, and this was his: coffee and dry toast.

It worked every single time.

He opened the kitchen doors and smiled as he saw Angel at the stove, flipping pancakes as well as frying some bacon.

"Have I told you I loved you lately?" he asked, going straight to the coffee machine.

Angel chuckled. "Don't let Lash hear you say that. He'd be so upset. He'd ban you from the club."

Ink wrinkled his nose. "I love you like a sister. You know that."

"Dry toast?"

"It's like you read my mind."

"I just remember what it is you consider to be the cure. I know it's different for everyone. For instance, Tate thinks boiled eggs does the trick. Lash, his is always black coffee. You know, I just remember these things. It's fun." She shrugged and then smiled at him. "Take a seat."

Ink sat down at the large table, and minutes later Angel put the dry toast in front of him, along with a second cup of coffee. He finished the dregs of his first cup and smiled as he started to feel instantly better.

Maybe it was being waited on, or he just had the magical cure. He finished the first slice of toast, sat back, and nibbled on the second as he drank from his cup of coffee.

"You heard from Darcy today?"

"Steven got in an hour ago. He's crashed. Alan has taken over for now. I believe Lash will be next. I'm packing up some goodies for him to take. She must be hating it there. I've also put together a care package with all of her favorite books, and look, I got a music player for her. I know she loves her music."

Ink got up and crossed the kitchen to where Angel had everything on display. "It looks good."

It did as well. The box was huge, and with Angel's flair for care, it had pink ribbons, some girly bracelets and necklaces, or at least they looked like crafting things.

"It looks good."

"Good. I want her to know she's still loved."

"Why wouldn't she think she's not loved?" he asked.

"Sandy mentioned how she was coping. She was going through all these emotions, and well, I don't want her to think we think of her any less than we do now. She will pull through this."

Ink was starting to see the problem.

Angel was nervous, and she was trying to pretend she wasn't.

He placed an arm across her shoulder. Lash would kill him, but he had absolutely no attraction to this woman.

"This is more than enough."

"I hope so." Angel breathed out a sigh of relief.

"Get your arm off my woman."

Ink laughed as he removed his arm and turned toward Lash.

"Oh, enough with you and your possessive attitude. Nothing was going on. Just me and Ink talking about my care package is all. You know you're going to scare all the members off and end up with a club full of women," Angel said, walking up to Lash.

"Nope, even women would touch you, and I wouldn't allow it." Lash pulled her in close. "I love you."

"I know you do, but stop." Angel kissed his cheek before pulling away and heading back to breakfast.

"I'll take this to Darcy if you want. I know you're busy with the kids and stuff." He looked toward Lash. "You can spend some time with her."

"You sure you want to keep going to see Darcy?"

"Look, I'm not some pervert. I care about Darcy, and I want to make sure she's okay."

"If you're happy to do it, then by all means, do so. Tell her we love her," Angel said.

So a couple of hours later, Ink was walking down

the main children's cancer unit. With the club funds, Darcy was in a private ward, being seen to by a private doctor.

He stopped outside of her door and saw her scribbling away at her notebook. Her school bag was on the floor, and on the bed was an assortment of books.

Lifting up his knuckle, he gave the door a knock, and waited for her to look up.

When she did, there was no smile that he was normally used to. In fact, she looked ... pissed off to see him.

She closed the book on her lap and pushed it away. "What is it?"

He entered the room, closing the door behind him, holding the care package. "Angel wanted me to bring you this."

"She did?"

"Yes."

"Oh." Darcy nodded and moved some of her books away, tapping the bed.

He moved closer, putting the box on the bed and waiting as Darcy opened it up. She rummaged through the wrapping, and he saw the edge of a smile to her lips.

"Books. Makeup. Tell Angel I love her." She opened up a box of the cookies, and without even consulting the doctor, she opened them up and took a bite. He watched her eyes close. "They are so good."

"Angel's cooking is the best."

"I can't wait to have one of her famous hot chocolates. I need one right now." Darcy moaned.

"How is everything going?"

"Okay, I guess. Not a whole lot is happening. I started my first round of chemo yesterday."

"And how does that feel?"

"Fine, I guess. I feel a little ... strange, but the

doctor said we take it one day at a time. We don't rush these things."

He noticed she seemed calmer today, not as volatile, which he was more than happy with. Grabbing the chair, he placed it closer to the bed, and took a seat.

"You like books?"

"Love them. They pass the time, and well, there's nothing quite like a romance story." She sighed. "Sorry, you must think I'm too girly."

"Not at all. I think it's nice how much you love to read."

There was silence, and he watched as she glanced down at her books. She looked suddenly nervous, biting her lip, before finally looking up at him.

"Can I ask you something?"

"What?"

"Do you think I'm pretty?"

He went from being comfortable, to feeling like an asshole in a short span of time. Darcy had never made him feel this way before, and he didn't want to upset her. "Darcy?"

She got off the bed, her hands behind her, thrusting her chest up. "I'm not trying to be a bitch or anything. I don't even know why I'm asking this. Forget it."

She looked so incredibly sad, and for a split second he thought about someone from his past. Someone he didn't talk about to anyone.

"I think you're pretty."

"You do?"

"Yeah." He wasn't mean. Darcy was a pretty girl. There was nothing wrong with saying she was pretty. With everything she was going through, he didn't want to add to it.

"Would you go out with me?" She took a step

away from the hospital bed.

"You're fifteen." He stood up, not wanting her to have the advantage over him.

"I won't always be fifteen. I mean, I could be one of the rare few that dies."

"Don't do this," he said, seeing where she was going with this and not wanting to be part of it. "You're underage, and you're sweet, but I'm not going to go there."

"Go where? We're just talking, Ink?"

"You're upset," he said.

"Why? Because I got cancer? Is it so wrong for me to ask some questions?" she asked. "You know I like you."

"Darcy, it's a crush, and you're going to get better."

"People die every single day from cancer." She stood right in front of him. "I could be dead without ever knowing what it's like to really be alive."

"Darcy?"

"My parents keep me so protected because of the club. No guy is ever going to ask me out. Dad would kill anyone who came close to me."

"Your parents love and protect you."

"What if you could give me my first kiss?"

"That's not going to happen." He caught her wrist before she could touch him. "I've got to go."

"I've made you uncomfortable."

"Darcy, you're underage. You know for kissing you I could end up on a fucking registry, let alone what the club would do to me. I care about you. You're a club kid, but that is all. I've got to go. Killer is taking over."

"I'm sorry. Please, you don't have to go. I'll be good. You don't have to leave," she said.

"No, Darcy, I don't want to hear it. I get that

you're pissed off and angry for what is happening to you, but that doesn't give you the right to make me feel this way." He held her hands in his. She looked so small and fragile against him, and what she was going through, he couldn't begin to imagine. This was all too much, and with each day that passed she was only going to get worse. "You're a special girl, Darcy. Amazing, and I know one day you're going to make a guy really happy. You're going to fight this. I have a few other things to do today."

"Ink, wait."

He left the room, closing the door behind him. The sick feeling in his stomach came back in full force.

Killer just happened to be coming around the corner as he left the room.

"You okay?" Killer asked.

"Not in the least. I've got to head back to the clubhouse." He left without another word to Killer. He pulled out his cell phone even before he left the hospital, dialing Lash's number.

"What is it?"

"I can't help watch Darcy anymore."

"What does that mean?" Lash asked.

Ink gave Lash a rundown of everything that happened in the bedroom. For Ink, he knew people would think he was overreacting, and maybe he was, but he knew Darcy had a crush on him. He'd seen the signs, and even Emily had told him. With her being sick, he couldn't allow himself to be pulled into that mess. What if she didn't make it? What if everything failed and she asked him to do something that went against all of his principles? He didn't want to be the one to reject her or to hurt her further. She was so young, and with everything she was going through, he couldn't do that to her.

"Okay, I understand."

"No, I don't think you do," Ink said.

"What are you saying to me then?" Lash asked.

"I want to head to Piston County for a time." It just came out of the blue in his mind. He couldn't think of anything else to do. If he was anywhere near Darcy, there was a risk, and he couldn't allow himself to hurt her. This was for the both of them.

Piston County was where the Chaos Bleeds MC resided, and they were run by Devil. They also happened to be The Skulls' closest allies, and they had shared more death in the past ten years than any other club combined.

"You don't want to wait this out? She hit on you one time. It'll pass."

"No, I want out of this. I don't want to hurt her, and I don't want to be put in a position like this. I need to do this, and if you were the one being flirted with, you'd understand." Ink had seen enough death in his life. He wasn't willing to risk seeing anymore, but he also wasn't willing to risk Darcy doing something she would regret later, or putting himself in a position to hurt her.

Chapter Three

Three weeks later

Darcy felt sick to her stomach. The chemo was working, and her hair was starting to fall out in clumps. She couldn't bring herself to shave her hair off though. She was hoping her hair would remain. She felt sick all the time, tired, and now she had started to look it as well, even more so than when she was admitted to the hospital.

"And he's been gone ever since," Tabitha said. "Simon told me he doesn't even wear the leather cut anymore. It's a sign of respect for the Chaos Bleeds crew, but he's settled down." Tabitha popped her gum, getting to her feet to inspect the book titles on the cabinet beside the bed.

"So, he's just gone?"

"Yeah, I wonder what you said to him," Tabitha said.

"Why did I have to say something to him?"

"Come on, Darcy, don't be dense. You and I both know he came to see you before Ink just decided to leave Fort Wills. He loves this place and the club. This is his family. Whatever you said clearly spooked him. I checked his room at the clubhouse. It is empty. Just a bed remains. I don't know if Lash is going to let someone else take it. Probably. The club is always expanding, you know how it goes."

"No, I don't know how it goes," Darcy said. She was reeling. Ink was gone. The moment she asked him the question about if he thought she was beautiful she knew she had made a mistake. She'd also tried to stroke his chest and flirt with him. She'd seen him, and the fear of dying without at least kissing him once had struck her hard. What had she done? It was the only mistake she'd ever made, but it was a big one. She hadn't been able to get her stupid mouth to stay closed, and now, Ink was gone.

He'd gone to Piston County, to stay with Chaos Bleeds and to never see her again.

"Oh, shit, you're crying," Tabitha said.

To her amazement, she was. The tears wouldn't stop. They were falling thick and fast. She felt sick to her stomach, so emotional and overwrought. It was too much for her.

"I'm sorry. You're right. It's all my fault."

"I didn't exactly say it was your fault. I said you probably did or said something, and well ... please, don't cry. I hate that I made you cry. We're supposed to be besties, and we don't make each other cry."

Darcy covered her face. "I asked him if he thought I was beautiful. Ugh, I even tried to touch him as well. He looked really uncomfortable. This is all my fault. I'm a horrible person."

"I think that's a bit much, but you actually asked him that?"

"Yes. I don't know what was going on inside my head. I can't believe I'm even thinking about this right now. I was flirting with him. Me. I didn't pretend I didn't want him. I'm such an idiot." She sniffled, hiccupped, and then began to sob.

"Oh, no. Please stop. If you don't the nurses will send me on my way, and we won't be able to hang out in here anymore."

"I'm supposed to be going home soon, but Ink's gone. How can Ink just go like that? Am I so horrible?"

"Tell me what happened," Tabitha said.

Darcy struggled to explain everything. She had felt really shitty and horrible. Then Angel had sent that care package and Ink was there. For her, it had been fate, like Ink was supposed to be there for her. Only, it hadn't exactly ended that way.

"Wow," Tabitha said. "You really just tried to put yourself out there."

"I know." She couldn't believe she was unloading on her much younger friend. "I'm sorry. I know you want to be away from school and not worry."

"It's not that. Don't worry about that. I'm here for you because I adore you. School is not the same without you. Now that Sally is with Steven all the time, it's just different. Everything is all falling apart, and people are growing up. I hate it." Tabitha hugged her.

Darcy knew her friend was holding back. The hugs were not as tight as she remembered. "What should I do?"

"You don't do anything. Ink has gone, and I imagine it's to keep himself safe as well. You *are* only fifteen. None of us really know his story. He's kind of been an enigma all the time he's been here. That's what Adam says anyway. You know what he's like."

She nodded.

Tabitha sighed. "Do you love him?"

"I don't know. I don't even know what love is. I'm so confused. Do you know what love is?"

"Of course, silly."

"How? You've only known Simon, and I know you two think you're destined to be together, but this is the real world. He doesn't live around the corner. How can you expect him to wait for you, or to do any of that?"

Tabitha popped her gum. "You really don't have any faith in anything, do you?"

"Look at me."

"I am looking at you. You don't need to get pissy at me because of what is going on. With Simon it's different, okay? It's real. It's everything. We complete each other, and I know he'd never do anything to hurt me. We love each other, and we're going to make it work. Either I move to be with him, or he'll move to be with me." Tabitha shrugged.

"You know I get a call every single time you're not in school."

They both jumped and looked toward the door where stood Eva, Tabitha's mother.

"Mom," Tabitha said.

"You were supposed to be in school. You promised me you wouldn't be a problem like this anymore."

"Mom, I'm not doing anything wrong. I'm with Darcy."

"Who should be resting. Hey, dear."

"Hi, Eva," Darcy said.

"Out, now. Out to school. Your father is downstairs, and he's going to personally escort you to school."

"Please, as if that will bother me," Tabitha said.

"You think it's going to look cool for you with your father taking you to school?" Eva asked.

"You think I'll care?"

Tabitha was out of the room before Eva could say anything more.

"I swear, that girl gets more mouthy as the years go on." She smiled as she looked at her.

"I'm sorry. She wasn't doing anything wrong. Just keeping me company."

"I know, sweetheart, but Tabitha still needs her education. She doesn't know everything yet, even if she does think it." Eva put her bag on the chair and walked toward the bed, tutting. There were some candy wrappers on the floor. Eva picked them up, placing them in the trash. "So, how is everything with you?"

"I'm fine. The same. You know."

"I know." Eva kissed her on the head. "We're all missing you back at home."

"You do know kids can go home in between treatments."

"We know. Your parents, they want what is best for you."

"And what is best for me is to stay inside this hospital room." They hadn't come to see her all that much since she arrived. They were there, but they didn't linger in the room. They'd kiss her head and quickly go and find the doctor. She couldn't help but think they were avoiding her.

"You're sitting with me today?" Darcy asked.

"I think so, yes. If you'd like the company."

"I'd be happy with it."

There was nothing else for her to do or say. This was her life, for the next couple of months, or even years.

Ink was gone, and she was all alone. Apart from Tabitha, but her young friend had to live her own life, while she remained locked away here. Sitting back, she listened to Eva read to her, wishing to be elsewhere, somewhere far away, with a beach, and where cancer wasn't even a word.

****

"You settling in okay?" Devil asked, entering the main warehouse for the old ladies' clothing store.

Ink put down his pen as he was going through the stock, which was what he'd been asked to do. He didn't mind being at the clothing store. After giving Lash his leather cut, he'd hightailed it out of Fort Wills and not stopped until he got to Piston County.

"Yeah, I seem to be. The girls don't have a problem with me working here, do they?"

"Nah, Lex thinks it's great. She wanted someone to help carry around the boxes, and well, guys have a reputation to protect."

"You trying to say I look like a girl?" Ink was more than aware of his masculinity. He had nothing to prove and nothing to hide either. He didn't mind working in a fashion shop, or even dealing with feminine hygiene products. He was a guy that knew work had to be done, and if there was a payday at the end of it, so be it.

"Well, you're sitting around a bunch of girly clothing. Tell me why you'd rather be working here than wearing your patch back at the clubhouse? That's what I don't get."

Ink looked down at the paperwork, shaking his head. "I've got to get back to work."

"Lash told me that Darcy made you uncomfortable."

Ink paused, staring down at the box filled with the latest fashions about to go in the shop.

"It had me wondering why a guy like you would feel the need to run from a fifteen-year-old girl."

"I'm not getting into this. You got a problem with me being here, I'll leave."

"I don't have a problem with you being here, Ink. I want answers to my questions. I don't like all the vague bullshit."

"And why should I give them to you?" Ink asked.

"This is my town. This is my family. I know you're a good man, and I'm not looking at a pervert who can't handle a young girl. There is something more here, and I want to know what it is." Devil straddled a chair. "We're alone. I get you don't want Lash and the others to know. I'm not part of the club."

"And you don't go telling shit to Lash?"

Devil laughed. "Son, I don't give a flying fuck how Lash handles his business. It's his business. It has nothing to do with me. You're in my territory, so the entire scheme of things changes a lot more. Sit the fuck down and tell me what your problem is."

Ink dropped back into the chair and glared at Devil.

"You think I'll get bored of this? I can do this all day, and will probably do it all day with my kids and their attitude. Now be a man and fucking grow a set. What has you running from Fort Wills?"

Ink didn't want to talk. He wasn't the kind of guy to share his thoughts or his feelings. "I can't get out of this."

"Not on my watch. Maybe if you were back home, it would be a whole different story. You're not at home though. You're in my town, and now I want answers."

"I'm not a bad guy."

"I know you're not. In fact, I don't doubt you'll return to The Skulls when you're ready. They will expect you back. You worked too hard for your patch to just throw it away."

Ink ran a hand down his face, trying to think of something, anything, that would get this asshole off his case. Rather than lie, he decided to go for the truth. There was nothing else for him to lose.

"I've … seen … fuck!" He got to his feet. "Darcy's not the first kid I've seen go through something like this. Only, the other person I knew, she didn't have amazing odds, not like Darcy."

"Who was it?"

Ink stared at Devil, gritting his teeth. "She was my baby sister."

"I didn't know you had a baby sister. I thought you always said you didn't have family."

"I don't have any family. She was ten, and I don't talk about her. I thought I had my shit together. Darcy doesn't need that around me. Not when she looks at me like I'm a hero. I couldn't save my sister, and I can't play the hero again. I've not got what it takes. People can call me a coward, but I don't give a fuck. I can't do it. Not now."

There was silence after his confession, and he couldn't bring himself to look at Devil.

"Why haven't you told anyone about this before?"

Ink burst out laughing. "I left all of that bullshit behind when she died. Everything else I talked about, I made up. I don't want any fucking reminders of the past. The Skulls, Fort Wills, it was supposed to be about moving forward. Not moving back. I've got to keep on going, and the only way to do that is to leave everything else behind."

"Darcy's diagnosis opens up these wounds?"

"Yes," he said, through gritted teeth. "It makes it even worse because of the way she looks at me. I'm no hero, and I can't save her. I'll never be able to save her. Not only that, she … she's fifteen. She's had a crush on me for the longest time. I don't want to hurt Darcy, but I'm not going to be the guy she comes to for pleasure. She is going through all this shit, and I just know—if not today or next week, one day she's going to want my kisses, then for me to touch her, and I'm not a monster. I don't want this to lead to anything else. I care about her but not enough to break the law."

"So you run away."

"Yeah, I guess that makes me a coward." He got up, running fingers through his hair, feeling sick to his stomach.

"I think a man knows when he's done too much and seen too much, and when it is best for all parties to get the fuck out of there. You've done what you had to do, and I'm not going to judge you for it. I heard what happened with Darcy, not all of it, but I've seen some of the teenage girls in town. The way they look at my men. It's dangerous, and they're not club kids. I can't imagine it's easy to handle rejection. Especially when it comes to Darcy and what she's dealing with. You're welcome to stay here for as long as you like," Devil said, slapping him on the back as he got up to leave.

Ink watched him go before returning his attention back to the items of clothing waiting for him to mark off. He tried not to think about his sister. It always left him with a bad taste in his mouth, and it was always something he wanted to avoid.

She'd been sick for a long time before his parents had finally sought treatment for her. They thought she'd been faking it. By the time they found the cancer, it had spread so badly there was no chance of her ever surviving. Within a year of her diagnosis, she was gone.

He thought about Darcy, the way she looked at him when she asked if he thought she was pretty.

He wasn't a good man, or a nice one. He did what he had to do, and after losing his sister, he'd taken it upon himself to cause as much fucking trouble as he could, until he heard about The Skulls. Once he found out about them, they gave him focus, drive, and a constant need to do better, to be better. He'd found his place, and just as soon as he realized it, he'd had no choice but to run away.

"You okay?"

He looked up to see Sasha, Pussy's old lady, as she came into the doorway. She had once been blind, but after an accident, her sight had miraculously returned.

"Yeah, I'm fine."

Ink didn't know if he'd ever be fine again. This thing with Darcy had already fucked him up, and he wasn't the one having to undergo treatment. She was. Rubbing the back of his head, he got to work, ignoring the inquisitive look on Sasha's face. She would need to realize there were a lot of men who wouldn't talk constantly about their feelings.

What Ink did do, was send a little prayer for Darcy. He hoped she was safe and pulled it through this, but it wouldn't be with him. He'd already failed to be someone's hero, and he wasn't going to do it again.

Chapter Four

Three years later

Darcy stared at her reflection in the mirror. She'd turned eighteen six months ago, but now, she was finally getting a party. There was no doubt there was cause for celebration. After three long years, she had finally been given the chance to call herself cancer-free. She would have to undergo regular tests in case her cancer came back, but the doctors were hopeful she'd made a full recovery.

She ran her fingers through her short hair.

Her hair had been completely gone during one stage of the chemo, and it had eventually grown back. It wasn't as long as it was, and she wasn't the same person.

She'd been a chubby kid, and prior to her diagnosis she'd weighed a lot more than she did now.

The chemo, the medication, all of it had lost her most of the curves she'd been more than happy with.

"Seriously, you look beautiful," Tabitha said, dropping onto the bed. She wore a pair of jeans, a long vest shirt that held a single rose in the center, and it looked like the rose was bleeding, and a leather jacket. She also wore trainers that looked like they'd seen better days.

No matter how pretty people tried to dress Tabitha up, she always went back to the same kind of clothing, practical.

"Aren't you going to get dressed?"

Tabitha rolled her eyes. "I've got it all waiting for me in your closet. Mom picked it out for me. Don't worry, I won't spoil your party by looking like me."

Darcy laughed. "You know I don't have a problem with the way you look."

"I know, but it's so … delicate." Tabitha got to

her feet and walked to the closet. "Look at this. There's no way I can even get away with running out of the party." She pulled out a white lace dress. It was beautiful, feminine, and when Tabitha was in it, she looked like a delicate, beautiful woman.

The Tabitha who stood before her now was a fierce woman, a fighter.

"Do you think I look pretty?" Darcy asked.

The moment she did, Tabitha lost the attitude. Her scowl turned into a smile. "I think you look stunningly beautiful." Tabitha put the dress on the bed, walking over to her. "I'm so happy for you. We did it, together."

Tabitha had been her rock during the worst of the procedures and medications. It didn't take their families long to realize they were both helping each other. Tabitha wrapped her arms around her waist, resting her head against her back. "I don't want to lose you."

"I know."

In the last three years, she'd gotten close to Tabitha, and to Miles, Daisy, and Anthony. They were the main group of The Skulls' kids. There were others, but they were the four main protectors, and the ones who upheld The Skulls' name.

Much to Darcy's shock, Tabitha had also put Michael in his place three years ago. She didn't know what exactly happened, but the guy did a complete U-turn, and had even graduated from high school, and was looking at college within the next year.

"You better get dressed," Darcy said.

There was a knock at the door, and Darcy called for them to come in. It wasn't surprising to see Daisy already dressed and ready. She wore a purple dress, one that fell to her knees.

All of the women, as per her request, were being

forced to wear a dress. She never got to go to prom or have a dance, and seeing as this was her party, she wanted it to be perfect.

"You two okay?" Daisy asked.

"Yeah, we're good. Can you help me with my zipper?" Tabitha asked.

Daisy nodded.

Darcy ran a brush through her hair as she watched the two girls by her bed. Tabitha stripped down and stepped into the white dress. They didn't know Darcy had been the one to pick all of the dresses.

Her mother had offered to help her, but Darcy wanted complete control.

There was another knock on the door as Tabitha was pinning up her blonde locks.

"Come in."

It was Emily, her mother.

"You look beautiful," she said.

Emily was dressed in blue. Darcy looked down at her own dress before offering a smile to her mother, who pulled her into an embrace.

"We'll leave you alone," Daisy said, grabbing Tabitha's hand and forcing her out of the room.

The door closed silently behind them.

"You spend a lot of time with Tabitha now."

"I know."

"So, you managed to graduate and you've been avoiding the college subject for some time now, Darcy," Emily said.

"You want to talk about that now?"

"I want you to know I'm here for you. That we're all here for you and whatever decision you make, we're all going to support it."

"I haven't made a decision yet."

"You haven't?"

"I don't know what I want to do." For a short time during her road to recovery, there were moments she really didn't think she was going to make it, and she thought about dying. What she'd done in such a short time had been nothing.

There was a chance the cancer could come back, and she didn't want to spend her life waiting for something like that to happen, scared of living.

She wanted to live. She wanted to do something with her life. Whatever it was, she didn't want to go to college, not yet anyway.

"I don't want to go to college," she said.

"You don't?"

"No. I don't. I'm not entirely sure what I want to actually do, but can I just have tonight where I don't think about the future and what it could mean?"

Emily nodded. "Of course." She got to her feet and pulled her in for a hug. "You have been amazing, strong and brave. You make me so proud."

Darcy held her mother, but again, she felt a little closed off from it all. There was no real connection there, and hadn't been for some time.

"Love you, Mom," she said. She did love her mother, both of her parents. But there was just something missing.

"I better head downstairs." Emily kissed her cheek one last time before leaving her alone.

Darcy sat on the edge of the bed. Her hands rested on her knees, and she hated as she thought about Ink.

He'd not returned in the three years he'd been gone. She wouldn't have made him uncomfortable. It wasn't her intention to do that. Whenever she thought about him, she always felt an unwavering sense of guilt and responsibility for sending him away. She never wanted to do that, and yet, she'd succeeded.

Getting to her feet, she didn't wear heels. Her balance had been off for some time, so she always wore flats.

Seeing no reason to linger in her room, Darcy opened the door, and sure enough, Drew was there. He'd gotten his patch a couple of years ago after helping out a couple of women who'd needed protection. He'd nearly died after taking a bullet to the chest, and because he'd put his life on the line for the women and for the club, he'd earned his patch.

"Hello," he said. "That's a good look for you."

"What? A dress?"

"No, the smile."

She put her fingers to her lips and rolled her eyes. "Of course, the smile."

"You've not been doing it a whole lot lately, and I've got to say, it doesn't suit you. You need to keep on smiling."

"You don't smile around Sally as much as you used to."

Drew laughed. "You know, I loved that girl, and I still love that girl, but I'm happy for her."

"You are?"

"You know it."

Drew had been in love with Sally, but her heart had belonged to Steven. There hadn't been a fight, not really. There was no way Drew would have ever won Sally's heart.

He offered his arm. "You want to head down together?"

"Why not?"

She was friends with all of The Skulls. Each one had come to her during her stays in the hospital. She had gone home a couple of times, but her sickness had only gotten worse. With a donation from The Skulls, she had stayed in a private room for more of her illness. Pushing all of those thoughts out of her mind, she took Drew's arm, and together they walked down the long staircase.

"You're beautiful," he said, leaning in close.

"Thank you." Drew was always a sweet guy, and she adored him. Even though she loved Sally and Steven together, she always felt sorry for Drew. He'd not moved on or found anyone else. She wanted him to find someone else, to be happy. He was a good guy, and he deserved someone who would love him how he wanted to be loved.

"Just so you know, Devil and some of his crew are here."

She was already aware because Tabitha had told her Simon was coming. "That's okay."

Drew paused before they entered the main clubhouse. "Ink's with them."

This made her heart skip, but she didn't have time to dwell before Drew was leading her into the throng of people. Everyone she turned to hugged her, and she saw the happiness in their eyes.

Getting the all clear was amazing news, and she was even happy by the fact she no longer had cancer. There would always be the chance it would come back, but she had to stop thinking about that. It would be a lot easier for her.

When Whizz pulled her into a hug, she let out a little yelp.

"Not so hard."

"We were all worried about you, kid, but so pleased to have you back." He went to ruffle her hair, but she quickly pulled away from him, wanting some space. She spotted Tabitha and Simon together, hanging out, along with Daisy and Anthony.

They were still younger than she was, and she couldn't keep hanging out with them.

Taking the fresh orange juice from her mother, she hugged her back.

"I'm so damn proud of you, baby," Emily said.

"Thank you, Mom."

Her father was next, holding her. "I love you, sweetheart."

"I love you too."

The love kept on pouring her way. Lexie and Devil held her close, and she laughed as Pussy and Sasha did the same.

Then after three years, she finally saw him.

Ink.

He stood by the bar, chatting with Steven and Lash. He looked … different.

Just from seeing him from the back, she could tell he wasn't wearing a leather cut, but the ink on his arms and the back of his neck was distinctive enough for her to recognize him.

When he turned around, she averted her gaze, heading toward Sandy, who was standing with Stink. Most of the kids were out by the play area, being watched over by a couple of brothers and old ladies. There was no room for club whores at a time like this.

"You okay?" Sandy asked.

"Yeah, I'm fine."

"I will go and get my lady another drink," Stink said, taking the empty glass from Sandy.

"Are you having a good time? Or are you just avoiding Ink?" Sandy asked.

"Why did he come back?"

"This is his home as well."

"Not for the past three years."

"I'm sure he has his reasons." Sandy touched her

arm. "What about you? How are you feeling?"

"The same as always, you know. I'm good though." The party wasn't how she imagined. She had expected to come downstairs and to just feel like herself before the cancer diagnosis, but instead, she felt … lonely. Incredibly so.

She kept trying not to look toward the bar when Stink came back. Making her excuses to the couple, she left the main clubhouse, searching for fresh air outside. After spending so much time in a hospital room, she preferred the great outdoors. She found herself now going out for long walks, and just spending hours either sitting near a tree, or just standing, staring up at the sky.

"Hello, Darcy."

She tried not to tense up, but his voice seemed deeper somehow. Rather than ignore him, she glanced over her shoulder at Ink. He'd not changed a bit. He'd gotten more muscles since she last saw him, and he seemed bigger, but other than that, nothing else had changed.

"Hey, Ink," she said, turning back to watch the club kids play. The playground had been installed years ago, and she recalled being a child and having the same kind of fun. It had changed throughout the years, and more area of the back of the clubhouse had been developed into a child's play area.

Lash had turned the club legit, and in doing so, he'd made it safer for all of them. There were no random shootouts, no nothing.

Just peace and quiet.

She knew most of the men and women preferred it that way.

"Are you just going to ignore me?" he asked.

"Last time I asked you any kind of question, you ran away. I figure if I keep my mouth shut, you won't have to keep on running anymore." She sipped at her drink, very aware of how close he stood beside her.

"I believe congratulations are in order. You beat it."

She smiled. "I did. How is Piston County?"

"It's fine. Not home, but I've been able to make a place there."

"Do you have anyone special in your life?" she asked. "Actually, scrap that. I'm just trying to make conversation. Being here with you makes me nervous, and well, I don't want to keep on talking about being ill. A couple of the nurses helped me learn some small talk while I was with them."

He chuckled. "It's fine."

"I didn't mean to make you run away," she said. "It wasn't about that. I just, I had a bad day."

"I know."

The guilt of forcing him from his own home still weighed heavy on her. "I didn't mean for you to leave Fort Wills, or to hand in your cut. I'm so sorry."

"I'm not seeing anyone, and it's fine."

"No, it's not fine. You shouldn't have to give up your whole life because of me. What I said was wrong and selfish."

Ink silenced her when he took her hand. "We can't take back what happened. You were young and scared, and I made the decision that was right. I could have told you how pretty you were, but you were fifteen. I didn't want to be put in that position. I had my reasons for doing what I did. I don't want you to feel guilty about this."

"But I do. If it wasn't for me, you wouldn't have left."

"Stop it. It doesn't matter anymore. What was done, was done. I don't want you to feel upset or guilty.

It's over, understand?"

She nodded.

With his hand touching hers, she felt so incredibly vulnerable right now. She had hoped that these feelings for him would have evaporated or disappeared. Instead, she felt even more in need of him, and it was driving her crazy.

"So, erm, are you heading back to Piston County after this weekend?" she asked, needing to put space between them.

"I don't know, to be honest. I thought I'd know what I wanted the moment I walked back into the clubhouse."

"You don't know?"

"I don't have a clue."

He shook his head. "I guess I'll just deal with what the future brings."

Chapter Five

"You know I can just give you back your leather cut, right?" Lash asked. "You didn't leave the club for being a pussy or anything. You had valid reasons. Just ask for it."

Ink laughed. "I'm not asking for it."

"Why not?"

"I don't deserve it. Not yet." He ran his fingers through his hair, looking out of the window into the main yard.

There was no denying he'd missed this, all of this. The family, all of it. Devil and Chaos Bleeds had a family, but they weren't The Skulls. They were just different. Being back here, he'd expected to know what he wanted out of life, but if anything, he was even more confused than normal.

"So, what are you going to do?"

"My old apartment is available. The last couple finished their rent a month ago, and well, I'm going to head out over there, fix it up, I think."

"You know your place is still here. The boys know why you left."

"No, they don't know the whole story, and I know I look like some kind of coward for running away."

"You don't look like a coward to any of us, Ink. You need to stop thinking like that. Darcy was young, and you did the right thing by leaving. No one knows what could have happened otherwise."

"I can live with the guys thinking whatever they want. For my cut, I need to earn it back. I left, and I haven't been part of the club for a long time. I think I should just stick around, you know, get used to being here again." He didn't know what the fuck he was saying.

"Are you okay?" Lash asked.

"Yeah, I'm fine. She made it through." He saw her sitting at the large picnic table, a small plate of food in front of her, surrounded by Tabitha and the others. They were all a happy family, a happy unit.

Only, he saw the sadness in her eyes, and he wished he knew how to make it better. Darcy wasn't anything like his sister.

He'd done the right thing. He couldn't forget what had led up to his leaving. It was for her own good and for his as well. She didn't need rejection on top of everything else she was going through.

He was stronger than this, dammit.

"My baby sister didn't get this chance."

When Lash didn't say anything, Ink turned to look at the other brother. "You're not going to ask me what I'm talking about?"

"No. I've known you for a long time now, Ink. I figured if something like this could make you run, there had to be other problems you were keeping to yourself besides the obvious, and I respect your decision for leaving. You did the right thing." He shrugged. "I don't make a habit of forcing the men to have a heart to heart with me if they don't want it. If you want to tell me, you will, and if you don't, you won't. It's simple as that, really. Darcy is a fighter, but something happened to her in the past three years. She's not the same kid I remember who'd laugh so easily or play pranks. In fact, if there are pranks being played, she's gone. Usually at home, or near a tree somewhere, reading. That's what she does a lot, read."

"You think it's because I left her?"

"No, I don't. I think with Darcy mistakes were made and she's lonely. I don't know. You're sticking around."

"Yeah."

"Well, it'll be nice to have you around, even without wearing the leather cut."

Angel walked into the office as Ink took his leave. The brothers didn't seem to hold a grudge, and for that, he was thankful. They had a right to be angry at him, pissed off, but at least they weren't openly hostile toward him.

The day wore on, and as night fell, the food was packed away and the kids were either taken home or sent to bed.

The boys and the old ladies hung out around a fire.

Ink made his way outside, watching them. Angel sat on Lash's lap. They weren't kissing, but just the way they held each other, he saw the love between them, shining brighter than any light.

Devil was the same, only Lexie straddled his waist and they were making out.

Tate and Murphy were together, as were Whizz and Lacey.

Seeing them all together, he felt this yearning deep inside him, and he took off out of the clubhouse.

Fort Wills wasn't an overly large town, but it had a lot of space.

Up ahead, he caught sight of Darcy. She'd changed out of her dress and was wearing a pair of torn jeans and a large sweater.

She'd lost a lot of weight, almost looking gaunt, and he didn't like that. From what he'd seen her eat, she wasn't eating enough.

It's not your business.

He followed her, keeping a good few feet from her, but making sure she never left his sight.

This was unusual, her being alone, and anyone

could come and take her. He didn't like it. The club should have known she snuck out.

At one point, she stopped and turned, looking down toward him, but never seeing him. He stayed to the shadows, which was always easy for him.

When she kept on walking, he followed her. She made her way into town, passing several of the shops, and even the graveyard. He made the sign of the cross over his chest, and sent a prayer up to all the lost and dead Skulls that had passed over the years. He had a habit of doing this, just so they knew someone was still thinking about them, still caring, and wanting them to be safe.

She wasn't immune to people wanting to hurt her, so the fact she was out on her own irritated him.

He followed her out to an old park, and she took off through the woods. She pulled out a torch to help her find her way, and he couldn't just leave her alone, and he wasn't about to call for help either.

If she wanted to be alone, she could be, but he'd also be here in case she needed him. When she came to a large tree—he didn't know what kind—she stopped, and he watched her as she began to climb it. The flashlight hung from a clip on her jacket.

In no time at all, she was sitting against the main trunk, and he heard her sigh out.

"You didn't have to follow me," she said. "I'm perfectly safe."

"You knew I was following you.

"I saw your shadow on the buildings."

"Why didn't you make me stop?" he asked.

"I don't know. It seemed like a waste for you to follow me over here and for me to just stop you from getting what you want? You were curious. Why?"

"Does your family or any of the Skulls know

you're out?"

"Technically, you're a Skull, so I'm guessing yes."

"I'm not a Skull, Darcy."

"Then nope, no one knows, but don't worry, I tend to be back before morning."

He rubbed the back of his head, trying to think of something logical to say to her, and he kept drawing a blank.

"Darcy, this is not safe."

"I've been doing this for a couple of weeks, even longer when I wasn't stuck in the hospital or being watched twenty-four hours a day. I don't mind. I like it here, and it's not cold. I can't come when winter hits. It's nice in the fall though. The leaves are on the ground, rustling along, and I can hear anyone who wants to try and sneak up on me." She pointed at the dry leaves on the ground close to him. "Why follow me?"

"You know you shouldn't be here on your own."

She sighed. "You're going to be a drag on my buzz."

"You're taking drugs."

"Hell, no. I've been on so many drugs, I don't want to take anything else, and I don't. Whenever I'm in pain, I'll deal with it. I don't want any more drugs in my system."

"Then what hell kind of buzz you're talking about?" he asked.

"Just listen and stop invading my damn space."

"I'm all the way down here."

"And yet, you're still invading everything. Shut up and listen."

"Fine. Fine." He stood silent, down on the ground, listening.

At first, he heard absolutely nothing, and then a

bird chirped faintly. The hoot of an owl, followed by the rustling of the trees, and it was actually incredible.

"See, you can hear it now. It's just nature. You know, no phones, no cars, just life, and it sounds amazing. It sounds like everything and nothing all at once."

He moved toward the tree and began to climb.

"What the hell are you doing?" she asked.

"I'm going to come and see you."

"No, Ink, this is my time and my space."

"And this is my life as well, and seeing as I'm here and I'm admiring *nature* with you, I get to make a decision here." He moved past her and sat on the really thick branch. It was an old tree, one that had clearly seen hundreds of years.

"This is my time. My space."

"And now you get to have company in your time and in your space."

"Don't do this."

"Don't do what?" he asked. "Talk to you? See you? Have some fun? I'm not going to hurt you, and in case you didn't notice at the party, I didn't exactly belong."

"That was your choice. Not mine. I didn't mean to make you leave by what I did. I had no intention to let it play out the way it did."

"You did though, and I don't want to keep going over this. Why can't you let it go?"

"Because I messed up. I did something wrong and selfish. I had just been told I had cancer. My hair was falling out. I felt horrible. I don't know why I asked you, you oaf. You don't have to keep looking for me. Get off my tree, dammit. This is my time. I won't have you invading it. You don't have to stick around. You can leave."

He glared at her, seeing the anger in her eyes, but he wasn't going to run.

"No, I'm not going anywhere."

"So, do you think I'm pretty, Ink?" she asked. She batted her eyes at him.

"Yes."

"Whatever. Will you be my first kiss? Will you love me?" She kept firing questions at him, and he took the flashlight from her hands.

"You still got a crush on me, Darcy? Do you still want to be my girlfriend?" he asked, taunting her back.

"So, going to Piston County grew you some balls."

"You've been hanging around Tate too much," he said.

"Ha, I don't hang out with Tate. That's all Tabitha."

"I shouldn't be surprised." He wasn't. Tabitha was a damn strong woman, even as a teenager. There was no one tougher than she was. She was a Skull through and through, even more so than Tate.

She didn't take shit from anyone, and through getting to know Simon, she was more than happy to fight for the club. Anyone saying bad shit always answered to her.

"If you hadn't run away, you'd know all of this and wouldn't need me to keep on telling you. Give me back my flashlight and leave."

He held the flashlight out of her grip. "I told you, I'm not leaving."

"I didn't come here to be harassed by you." She looked like she wanted to shove him, but he held his ground, refusing to budge, and she didn't touch him. "Please, leave."

"Not going to happen."

"Why do you have to be a pain in the ass?"

"Why do you have to be alone?"

"I like being alone. Didn't you hear? I spend a great deal of my time alone. This is who I am now. This is what I do." She folded her arms beneath her breasts, but he saw the pain inside her.

Alone she may be, but she didn't want it to be so.

****

Spending time with Ink wasn't what Darcy wanted to do. He'd left three years ago, and other than a rare visit when she was nowhere around, he'd stayed gone.

"Why can't you just go? You see I'm not hurting anyone."

"I know, but I don't want you to be alone. I've got nowhere else to be."

"So I'm pity company?"

He chuckled. "That's a good one."

"It wasn't supposed to be a joke."

"I know. It's still funny." He winked at her.

She didn't like that her attraction was still there. Staring past his shoulder out into the night, she knew he was watching her. There was a little thrill to finally have his attention, but even so, he'd ruined it by leaving.

"What are you plans now? You graduated high school even after all you'd done."

"Look, I know you're trying to play the nice guy and all that, but I'm really not interested, not even a little bit."

"I'm not playing any role here. I'm being the good guy because that is what I am."

She looked at him. "Seriously? You're going to say you're a nice guy."

"I'm one hell of a guy."

She laughed. "Oh, please, I asked you a simple

question, and maybe touched you a little, and you left. What did you think I was going to do? Jump your bones?"

"Nah, not that." The smile on his face disappeared.

"What is it?" she asked.

"Besides the usual problems a fifteen-year-old coming onto a much older guy would have, you reminded me of someone I used to know. Well, I can't exactly say reminded me of, but the circumstance did."

"What were they?"

He shook his head. "It doesn't matter. It's over now, and you're officially cancer-free."

"I've got to keep getting tests. It's only after a period of time that they give you a cancer free. Every time I yawn, Mom looks like she wants to phone the doctor or something." She smiled, but even she knew it didn't quite reach her eyes.

"That bothers you, doesn't it?"

"A little bit. A lot, actually. I'm not sick and I won't always be sick, but they seem to think that's all I am. I'm not, I'm so much more." She sighed.

Silence fell between them, but she couldn't bring herself to look at him. With her attraction still there, she didn't want to make a fool of herself.

"Are you going away to college?" he asked, breaking the silence.

"No. I don't know if I want to waste time on college."

"How could that be a waste?"

"There is a chance this could come back, you know. I don't want to risk feeling like I've wasted even a single moment." She rested her head back against the tree. "It's why I come here. There's no one around to wait for me, to ask me questions. I can just think."

"Only now I'm here. So tell me, Darcy, what is really bugging you?"

"That you're here invading my thinking time."

"Besides that?" he asked.

"I don't know. A lot of things, I guess. I've been given this chance, and I feel like I'm expected to do other things, and I want to live a little. I want to go out all night partying, just to have the memory. Not to get sick, but not go in by curfew. Maybe get a job and live my own life. I don't think I want to live with my parents anymore." She pressed a hand to her mouth as she blurted those words out. "Please, don't say anything."

"Why would I have to say anything?"

"They're my parents and I love them so much, but I need space. I haven't had any space in so long, and I don't want them to be hurt."

"Sometimes you've got to hurt others to get what you want," he said.

"Ugh! Why do you have to sound so right all the time?" She laughed, leaning back against the tree. "Is that what you did with me?"

"I had to leave in order to save myself, yes. With you I was incredibly selfish," he said. "I'm so pleased you were able to fight this … disease."

She reached out, taking his hand, trying to offer him support. It was hard to stay mad at Ink. Deep down, she knew he was a good guy, even if he did run from her.

"I'm sorry for all that you've suffered before this. I didn't mean to make you run away from your home."

He placed his hand over hers. "Don't worry about it. You were young, and I was the grownup. You've got nothing to apologize for. I should have been stronger."

She sighed.

"You really didn't want to do this tonight," he said.

61

"I'm pleased you're back, Ink. Will you be sticking around?" she asked.

"I will be. I stopped renting my place out, so I'm going to be sticking around. I haven't taken my leather cut back. In all honesty, I don't feel I deserve it."

"Why not?"

"I left, Darcy."

"Don't. That was my fault, okay? I never got the chance to apologize for what I did. I … I'm sorry. Please. Don't do this. You have a right to be a Skull."

"I know what you're saying, but for me, I still left. No matter my reasons, for me, I need to earn it back. It doesn't make sense to a lot of people, but it does to me. I'll take my cut when I earn it back." He gave her hand a little squeeze. "I'm just not wired that way."

"But you earned it before. I don't see why you can't just, you know, have it again." She shrugged. "It was my fault you left last time. Don't worry, I'm not going to do anything stupid or selfish like that again."

"You have a boyfriend yet?"

"Nope. I'm still single. I don't know, I think it's the whole cancer thing. It makes men run in the opposite direction."

He chuckled as she looked at him with a scared face and showed men running away with her fingers as an example.

"At least I can get you to smile. That's a plus. Maybe you can hook me up with a friend or something." She winked at him.

"That is not happening."

She sighed. "I'll die a spinster."

"You'll find the right guy for you, Darcy. You've just got to be patient."

"I hate that word. Patient. I've been a patient, and now I've got to actually be it. It sucks."

"You can't spend the rest of your life in a tree," he said.

"True, but then, I have no intention of spending the rest of my life in a tree. Just a couple of hours."

He watched her as she looked out across the distance, clearly lost in her own thoughts. The night wore on, and Ink didn't rush Darcy. They both stayed silent, and he gave her the peace and quiet she deserved. No one stopped by or asked them to leave.

The tree was rather private, and as he watched Darcy, he noticed she didn't look tired. Glancing down at his watch, he saw they'd been sitting in the tree for nearly two hours.

"It's time for me to head back. If I stay too long, I'll fall asleep and that wouldn't be good," she said.

Ink climbed down first, waiting for Darcy. When she got to the last part, he gripped her waist, noting how slender she'd gotten in the past three years.

She thanked him, stepping away from him the moment her feet touched the ground, and brushed the bark from her hands.

"You want to walk me home? I can text my parents that I didn't want to stick around. They'll understand," she said.

"If that's what you want."

"Don't worry. I have no intention of hitting on you or flirting."

"I'll walk you back to your place." Guilt was a horrible thing, and he was feeling it right now with Darcy.

"You know, I remember when you would blush and pretend not to be able to talk to me," he said.

"Please, don't bring that up. It was a stupid crush. One I really shouldn't have had." She shrugged. "Can we call truce on the whole thing? Just be friends?"

"You have room in your life for one more friend?"

"I have a room for a lot of things. In case you didn't notice, my best friend happens to be Tabitha, and she's still in school. I didn't exactly blend well with my peers, and seeing as I spent the last couple of years in and out of the hospital, I didn't exactly make any real connections. Besides, Michael is an asshole, and he probably screwed his way through most of my friends."

"So friends it is?"

"Certainly."

He held his out to her, and she took it.

"Friends," she said.

Ink gripped her hand a little too tightly, but when she pulled away, he let her go. Being her friend, it was the least he could do.

Chapter Six

One week later

Darcy sipped at her sweet tea and crossed out another job application. She'd just called them to find the waitressing job had been filled at a restaurant just outside of Fort Wills. She'd also struck a cross through jobs available at the church, the gym, and also the café in town, which was where she now sat, drinking really good coffee.

Her parents were busy working at their prospective jobs with The Skulls. What she wanted to do was a job away from the club. She didn't have a problem with The Skulls. They were her family, and she loved them.

What she really wanted to do was to spread her wings and to find something outside of the protective bubble they'd set up. Maybe even find a guy who would be willing to date her. She had a plan.

Find a job, get an apartment, and then go on random dates with guys she didn't know, without her parents or the club finding out. It sounded perfect to her. All she had to do was find a job and hope not to have every single Skull turn up to warn everyone away from her.

She found one for the dentist, but that would be a big no-no because of Kelsey, who was a dental nurse and also happened to be married to Killer.

The jobs that were available were either for a Skulls job, or one closely related to The Skulls.

Just as she was about to get up and leave, a coffee was placed beside her.

She turned to see Ink standing there. It was still weird to her to see him walking around without his leather cut.

"Hey, you," he said. "You look like you could use a drink."

"It's not the drink I need, but a job, a nice one with a big, fat paycheck." She took a sip of the coffee. "The coffee is nice though."

"I always live to serve." He took a seat, and she suddenly didn't wish to be anywhere else.

"You're job hunting."

"Yep, and it seems not a lot of jobs for inexperienced young people. It's so wrong." She spread open the paper, and it was with some effort she didn't burst into tears. This wasn't about crying or getting upset. She just wanted to try to make a life for herself now that she was better. "So, erm, you got any bright ideas?"

"You've crossed out all the jobs available that are associated with The Skulls. Why?"

"I want a clean start. I don't want people to be looking at me because I'm the daughter of a Skull. I want to earn my living properly. Is that so hard to ask?" She folded the newspaper.

"In case you didn't know, The Skulls run this place, and they touch everything. There's no way you're going to be able to find a job without at least alerting them first."

"Then I've got to move."

"Darcy?"

"What?"

"Don't you think you're acting a little rash here?"

"No. I think I'm acting just right. I want to make a life for myself away from everything." She sighed before taking a sip of her coffee. Maybe moving away from Fort Wills wouldn't be a problem. Wherever she went, no one would know her or her past.

She stared down at the newspaper and knew she

had to do some research.

"You're a genius, Ink." She dropped down off her seat, leaving the half-finished coffee as she headed out toward her home.

"Whoa, wait a minute. I can tell by the look on your face that what I've said and what you're actually going to do are two completely different things," Ink said.

"They are. I want a clean start. Away from all of this. The only way I'm going to be able to do that is by leaving Fort Wills behind. It's a perfect plan."

"Wait, wait, wait, you can't just leave."

"Why not?"

"You've got … aftercare and tests."

"All of which I can come back down do, but I have to do this. I've got to do something. Otherwise I'll go out of my mind. Why can't you see that?"

He gripped her shoulders, stopping her from moving anymore. "Calm down."

"I don't want to calm down, Ink. I want to do this."

"You want to completely abandon your family?" he asked.

She let out a growl. "No. I just want to be able to have a life. You know, some fun. Something where not everyone knows that I've just gotten over cancer and want to talk about it." Her face was heating up, and Ink nodded.

"I get it."

"You do."

"Yes, I do. Running away isn't going to change that though. It's a part of who you are."

She stopped and closed her eyes. "You're right." Without thinking about it, she gave Ink a hug before stepping back.

"You're not going to go and do something crazy?"

"Nope. I'm just going to go home and look for jobs, maybe even call a couple of them that I crossed out."

She let Ink go, very aware of her body and where he'd touched her. She shook her head, trying to clear the fog that only Ink seemed capable of making her feel.

Taking the shortest route home, she arrived just as her mother was leaving for work.

"Hey, honey, how was coffee?"

"Good, it was good."

Her mother kissed her head, telling her how much she loved her before heading out.

Darcy walked inside and found her dad, Blaine, leaning against the kitchen counter.

"Hey, sweetheart," he said. He held open his arms, and she stepped into them, hugging him back. "How was your morning?"

"Good. Good. I'm looking for a job."

"You know you don't need to worry about those kinds of trivial things, right? We'll take care of you."

"You're going to take care of me when I'm old and got a husband." She didn't mention the kids. There was no point. The doctor had told her there was no chance of her ever having children.

"Don't you know, I'll be taking care of you forever and ever." He kissed her temple. "So, you don't have to work too hard to look for a job. Just relax. You've been through a lot, and I don't want you having to worry about that stuff."

Again, he was trying to protect her and she totally got it and even liked it, but this was still her life and she needed to be able to have her own space.

"Thanks, Dad," she said. She didn't want to argue

with him.

He kissed her head again. "That's my girl. I've got to head out to work. You'll be okay on your own?"

"Yes, I will."

She waited for him to go before heading to the laptop. Firing it up, she typed in job searches for locations outside of Fort Wills. She was determined to have a life, even if that didn't mean it would be in Fort Wills.

****

Ink was putting on the finishing touches of his latest coat of paint. He was determined to completely change his apartment, to give it a new and fresher vibe, when his doorbell rang.

Blaine was on the other side of the door, and Ink frowned, opening it up.

"Hey, man, I thought you could do with a housewarming gift." In his arms was a coffeemaker.

"Wow, a coffeemaker. What could I possibly need with that?"

Blaine laughed. "Well, as you know I'm not a drinker, but this stuff is good for you. It'll keep you up at night."

"Come on in."

Ink moved out of the way to allow room for Blaine to enter. "The place is pretty empty."

"Yeah, the last people I had renting took all of their stuff."

"Wow," he said.

"It's not too bad. It means I get to start it all over again." Ink touched one of the dry walls before turning to Blaine. "This is the first time you've ever come to my place, and I can't help but wonder if you've got a reason for that," Ink said.

"You got me. I do have a question, or should I

say some advice, and I want you to be honest with me," Blaine said.

"Okay."

"Darcy, do you think she's happy?"

Ink paused and gave Blaine his full attention. "I don't know what is going on here."

"Look, all of my life I've always been blinded by shit. I'm not pretending to know anything here, but I know Darcy had a thing for you. I told you three years ago I had no hard feelings."

"Blaine, I don't like this. I'm not going to meddle."

"I want you to take my daughter out. I want you to befriend her and give her a reason to stay in Fort Wills."

At first Ink thought he'd heard incorrectly, but one look at Blaine, and that wasn't the case.

"What?"

"I know my daughter has a thing for you, or at least she used to, and I know she's going through a lot right now. I want to help her, I do, and I think the only way for me to help her is to let her have some fun at home."

"By asking me to help her make this decision for her?" Ink asked.

"No. I love Darcy. She has been through a lot. Emily and I know she's wanting a clean start. Something where no one touches her or does anything to hurt her, and we want that as well. But we also know she's craving her independence, and we want her to have that. Make no doubt about it, we do want her to experience it, but not like this. Not away from us or away from the club."

"You think I can do that?"

Blaine pulled out an envelope from his back

pocket.

"Dude, I'm not going to take your money."

"It's not money. Inside are keys to an apartment a couple floors above yours. We've rented it for Darcy. It's fully furnished, and there's also a job at the library. It's not a lot, but it's something. I've pulled some strings, and I want you to be the one to give this to her. To show it to her."

"You want me to lie to your daughter?" Ink asked.

"For her own good. She thinks Emily and I don't see a problem happening. We see it. We know she sneaks out at night. That she's not been the same since she was given the all clear. We see it all, and it's killing us that we can't reach her. As parents we want what is best for our daughter, and if it means coming to the guy she had a crush on throughout high school, I'm willing to do it."

"She no longer has a crush on me."

"You can't touch her, Ink. You can show her a great time but no touching. Nothing with hands, nothing."

"I wouldn't do something like that."

"No falling in love with her either. I don't want her to be confused by all that bullshit."

"What kind of person do you think I am?" Ink asked, taking the envelope from Blaine. It didn't sit well with him to lie to Darcy, but this did give her a chance where no one else did. "You can't tell her I'm part of this."

"I won't. Darcy will never find out. I just want her to have a life where she doesn't think her parents are constantly breathing down her neck." Blaine held out his hand. "Deal?"

"Deal." Ink shook Blaine's hand.

"You really need to get your leather cut on.

You're not doing us any favors with those fucking muscles constantly on display."

"Fuck off, Blaine."

"Remember, she can never know," Blaine said as way of goodbye.

Closing the door, Ink leaned against it, pulling out a set of keys from the envelope. He saw the apartment number, and wasting no time, he left his place, taking the elevator to go and check out Darcy's place.

Sliding the key into the lock, he opened the door, and lo and behold, there was Darcy's apartment. It was a small place.

A tiny sitting room, the shelves were empty, and there was also a television and some furniture. A small sofa, a cute dining room table, a kitchen, and he checked out the bedroom. It was a small one-bedroom apartment that was perfect for a single woman.

He could imagine Darcy living here, a sense of independence.

There was a spike of guilt about lying to her, but this was what she wanted, and if he could give her anything back, it would be this. He couldn't give her what she wanted three years ago. He also didn't want to hurt her, but at least he could do something now to make up for it. When he got the news she was cancer-free, he'd been so happy for her. He'd not been here in person, but he had hoped and prayed every single night for her.

Flicking the keys around his finger, he left, making sure to close up behind him, whistling to himself as he made his way back to his place.

He picked up the paintbrush and finished off where he started. Drawing the brush up and down, he painted over some of the horrible flowered wallpaper. It would have to have a couple of coats of paint to completely cover over everything.

Out of the corner of his eye, he kept looking at the keys. He'd also seen the application for the library. It wasn't one from the newspaper but a flier.

He couldn't go immediately to her with the news. She'd get suspicious. He'd have to take his time with this one, and make sure she didn't suspect he was working with her father.

Once he finished the last coat of paint, he grabbed himself a beer and took a seat to admire his handiwork. He still worked for The Skulls even if he didn't wear his leather cut anymore. For the past three years he'd kept his head down and worked his ass off for Lexie and her girls. Their company was becoming one of the places to be for fashion, especially for down-to-earth kind of women.

Women like Darcy.

Shaking his head, he got back up. That would be his last beer for the night because he had to keep his shit together.

****

Blaine climbed back into the car and glanced over at his wife. To think, all those years ago he could have lost her, and when he finally got her back, he'd never let her go, nor given her a reason to doubt him again.

Earning back her trust had meant everything to him, and there was no way he'd ever ruin their life together.

"Is he going to do it?" Emily asked.

"He took the keys from me. I'll take that as a pretty good sign. You sure this is the right idea?"

"Darcy's wanting to live her own life. We've seen this for a long time. It's only a matter of time before she eventually leaves, and I want her to have a good life. A happy one, and we know we can trust Ink. He'll protect her when we're not there."

"He's a lot older than she is."

"So. Relationships like that work."

"There's a bigger age gap than you and me."

"Are you getting really overprotective again?" she asked.

"No. Yes. Maybe. She's our little girl, Emily."

"I know, and our little girl wants to grow up, and that doesn't mean hanging around with her father and mother. This is a good thing."

"And if she finds out we meddled she'll be upset."

"She won't find out, Blaine. Stop worrying about everything. We've got this." Emily leaned over and kissed his cheek.

"The last time Darcy tried to tell Ink how she felt, he ran."

"He's not going to run now. Besides, it's not like they're going to be having sex and a physical relationship. We're talking about friendship."

He snorted. "Like those work."

"They have been known to, Mr. Smarty Pants. Come on, let's go."

Blaine started up the car and pulled away from the curb, smiling. He knew he'd done the right thing. He only hoped his daughter, if she ever found out, would see it that way.

Chapter Seven

"Ouch!" Darcy hissed as she stared down at her finger. A paper cut, and it stung so damn bad. Sticking the wounded digit into her mouth, she sucked the small droplet of blood and went back to looking over the newspaper job advertisements, and again, she was still crossing out possibilities and when she called, they no longer had any offers on the table. It had been nearly two weeks since she looked online to see if she could find accommodation elsewhere but to no avail.

Moving away from Fort Wills would have been a huge move for her. She didn't want to leave her home, but she did want to be independent.

"Coffee," Ink said.

"Thank you."

She pulled her finger from her mouth and took a sip.

"Still got nothing on the whole job front and apartment hunting?"

"I've got nothing. I did check everything out that you told me to, but it's a dead end. Also, I tried to see what was available outside of Fort Wills and nothing."

"So you're not leaving."

"I'm not leaving, and I'm not working. I can be, like, The Skulls' little princess or something."

"And this is really important to you. To have your life back like this?"

"It is really important to me, yes. I don't know how to explain it. I just know this is what I want and what I need. Maybe it is foolish of me. I just want to know what it's like to stand on my own two feet. I want to give my parents space, and I'd like to have my own. I'd also like to just be me, you know." She shrugged. "I'm sorry. I bet you've got more important places to be and what I'm talking about is really silly."

"It's not, and I do have something for you." She watched him as he pulled out a creased envelope and pushed it across the table.

"Is this one of those bad deals? I don't want drugs."

He chuckled. "It's not drugs."

"Are you wanting me to be a prostitute?" she asked.

"Just open the envelope."

"Is this a way of sealing the deal? I open this and you've got to kill me."

"I won't kill you. I won't even harm you. Please, open the envelope," he said.

She picked it up and looked inside. There was a set of keys and a creased, old looking flier. "Keys?"

"My apartment building happens to have a vacancy. I've already rented it out, and it's a pretty decent size and it's not overly expensive. Also, a job offer. Not all jobs come in newspapers."

"The library."

"You love books if I recall. It's not too taxing, and I don't think any of The Skulls visit there. You'll be free."

"But, how did you come by this if none of The Skulls go there?"

"I go there. I needed to get a book for some DIY purpose. I checked out how to do something, and there was the flier."

She stared down at the application. She could work around books. She didn't have any problem with them. Sure, they smelled, but it was the good, used book smell. It was incredible.

"And you've already paid the rent on this place?"

"Yes. I figured we could stop off at the library.

There are a few books I want to take out, and then we can go and see your new place. You can deal with your parents. I'm just helping out. You'll have your own space, and you won't be crowding mine." He held his hands out as if to ward her off. "I just thought this offered an amazing opportunity for you."

"It does. It really does." She giggled. "Oh my, I can't believe this. Okay, okay. First stop, the library, and then you're so taking me to this place."

She finished her coffee and felt a total buzz. Her life was looking up already, and she could totally handle this.

"Come on, please, please," she said.

Ink finished his coffee, and they both walked together, heading toward the library.

She went straight up to the receptionist's desk and he left to go and look for some book. After a twenty-minute interview, she got the job and would be starting the next day. Much to her surprise, Ink came to the desk with a bunch of books and a library card. He actually had a library card.

"I'll take these, please," he said.

She leaned against the counter, waiting for him.

Once he finished, he carried the books, his large, impressive arms seeming to bulge from the weight of them.

"You didn't think I had a library card, did you?"

"Busted. I thought this was something The Skulls had cooked up, but again, I don't know why they'd go to such lengths. It seems silly now." She was in a happy mood.

"Did you get the job?"

"I got the job." She pretty much screamed it. She quickly covered her mouth. "Sorry, overexcited here, and I nearly messed everything up."

He laughed.

"I'm sorry. Is there anything else you have to do today? I can go and see this place on my own."

"Do not even think about it. I'm coming with you to check your place out."

"Haven't you seen it?" she asked.

"Yeah, but I now want to see it with you. Seeing it by myself, I could only imagine what it is like for you."

"Okay." She walked beside him. Her very much younger teenage self would have been so happy in this moment. It would have been a dream come true to walk beside her one true crush.

All of that was gone now. She was just happy to spend time with him. Other than that one time in the hospital, he didn't have a judgmental bone in his body, and even that time at the hospital wasn't his fault. She had fucked up, not him.

"So, I was wondering if you were going to get your leather cut back?" she asked. He'd been so proud to get that leather cut and to have his patch. She didn't like the idea of him going without it.

"I will when I earn it back for me. I still work for The Skulls, and when I feel I've done what is right, I'll know."

She frowned. "I don't think you need to earn it back, Ink. I did talk to Lash. I told him it was my mistake."

"Lash knows everything. He's not holding my cut back, Darcy. I am. I don't want it back. I'm just not wired to take the easy route. You don't need to take the blame for me not taking the cut back. It's all on me."

"I am responsible," she said. "I don't know what came over me. I was in pain. I was hurting. Everything just seemed so hard, and I guess, seeing you, and you know, having that crush on you, I shouldn't have asked for anything or done anything. I'm sorry if I made you nervous."

"It's fine."

"Do you want me to carry any of those books? They look really heavy."

"I've got them, sweetheart."

"Ugh, don't call me that."

"Babe?"

"Not that."

"What should I call you then?" he asked.

"How about we stick to the good old reliable, Darcy?" She winked at him. "You know, I can enjoy that one."

"Darcy it is."

"See, that's not so hard." She was loving this. Spending time with him, talking—it wasn't flirting though, was it? No, she didn't think it was flirting.

They arrived at his apartment building, and they went to his floor first so he could drop the books off.

He put them down on a small table, and she waited for him in the doorway. Entering his home felt really … personal. She didn't know if he was ready for her to be in his space.

"You know this place won't bite you."

"I know. I know. It's fine. I just would really like to see this apartment."

He laughed. "Fine. Let's go and see it." He left his place, and they made their way up to her new place. There was enough distance between their floors that she didn't have to feel like she was living above him.

This was good.

Ink took the lead after the elevator came to a stop, and he leaned against the wall.

"This is it. Are you ready for this?" he asked.

"Ready as I'll ever be." She put the key in the lock, gave it a twist, and the door opened. Stepping into the apartment, she noticed it was small, but that didn't bother her. In fact, she was really charmed by the place.

It was ideal for a single person, and she knew what she'd fill the space with.

"It comes with furniture?"

"Yes, fully furnished. You've got to decorate it with your own personal touch, but I think this is incredible. What do you think?" he asked.

"Oh, my, and it's already rented." She walked toward the small bedroom, and through it was a tiny bathroom. She could totally see herself relaxing and having a lot of fun.

Rushing back out to the main room, Ink pointed at the door. "We can install some more locks for extra protection. This is pretty sweet deal."

"I want it. I, like, really, really want it."

"It's yours."

She screamed and threw herself into his arms. The moment she did, she tensed up and immediately stepped back. "I'm so sorry."

"Don't worry about it."

"Oh, my. I cannot believe this is even real right now. I can't wait to tell my parents. They are going to be so … they're going to hate it."

"Why don't you just talk to them? Explain everything and see what they do."

"You're right. I can't be afraid to do this, to move on." She nodded, tucking her short hair behind her ear. "I can't wait to go shopping with the first paycheck I earn."

This was going to be good.

She felt incredibly happy, and to have shared this moment with Ink, it felt right.

****

It took them all of three hours and one trip to move Darcy into her new apartment. Ink was shocked to discover she didn't have a whole lot of stuff. Her clothes were a small suitcase, and for most things, she would need to buy other items.

Blaine and Emily were playing their part well as they looked around her place. Lash and Angel were also there. Angel had made a care package for Darcy, which included all of the groceries she would need for a week, as well as to stock her cupboards.

"This is really something, sweetheart," Emily said.

Darcy placed a family photograph on the wall. "Isn't it? I know you want me to stay at home forever."

"No, of course not. We want you to be available and free," Emily said.

"That doesn't mean you're alone. Ink's in the building, and we are only a phone call away," Blaine said.

"I know. I know."

He saw the happiness in her eyes and the excitement. With the last box inside her small place, Ink watched her say goodbye to her parents. Angel and Lash also hugged her, and he was the last one to leave.

"Don't go," she said. "I mean, you can totally go if you want." She grabbed a knife and scored it across the tape over the box. He closed the door with Blaine giving him a warning to keep an eye on her.

She would never be alone. He would be here to protect her.

Walking back into the sitting room, he watched her pull out some books from the small box. Shoving his hands into his jeans pocket, he waited for her to finish what she was doing.

"Thank you so much for helping me today. Angel

made me lasagna. I've just put it in the oven. You can stay for dinner if you'd like? Be my very first dinner guest?" she asked.

"Sure. I'll also carry all the large boxes for you."

"We make a good team."

It was on the tip of his tongue to dispute that, but he didn't want to in any way ruin her happiness.

It took her thirty minutes to unbox her things, and he flat packed the boxes, putting them to one side as she went and checked the lasagna.

"Done," she said. "I don't have time to throw a salad together. Angel did make lemon pie though."

"Sold."

She chuckled. "This is all surreal right now. This is my own little place. Mom and Dad were happy. They seemed happy to you. That's not a bad thing, right, for them to be happy for me?"

"It's not a bad thing."

"Good. Good." She grabbed two plates, and he watched as she started to serve, using a butter knife and a dessert spoon.

"I think we're going to need to get you some kitchen things."

"I think you're right. I'm making a total mess of this. I'm so sorry." She put it on the plate and sighed. "Done."

She served him up, and seeing as Angel couldn't make anything bad, he dived in with relish.

Darcy took the seat opposite him. The table was small, intimate, and cute. He didn't want her getting the wrong impression.

So far, he'd not gotten the sense that she had a crush on him any longer, and it made him wonder if she ever would. Not that he wanted her to fall for him.

She was way too young, and besides, she was

finally getting her life back.

"What are your plans for tomorrow?" he asked. He needed to distract himself because right now, he was close to losing his freaking mind.

"I need to go shopping. I've got my job to go to. I can't wait to get started. I think afterward I'll go to the supermarket."

"How about I join you?" he asked.

"At work?"

"No, I'll walk you to work, but I'll join you at the supermarket."

"You really don't have to do that."

"I'm not going to do it forever. I'm worried about you, Darcy. This is all new. Believe me, I'd have loved to have someone willing to help me out the way I am with you."

"Really?"

"Yes."

"Okay, sure. I'd love the company, I guess."

"Will you be visiting that tree anytime soon?" he asked.

"No, not anytime soon. This place will give me the peace I need, I think." She took a bite of her lasagna. "Thank you for all of this. For helping me. For finding this place and my job."

"You haven't even been to your job. Hold off on the thank-yous, just in case you can't stand it."

She laughed. "I'm surrounded by books. I can't wait."

"Did you read a lot of books?" he asked.

"In the hospital I did. It took the time away from everything else. Tabitha was with me as much as she could be, but she ended up being escorted to school and one of the guys always checked to make sure she stayed in class."

"I bet she loved that."

"Not even a little bit. She got into a lot of fights, but I think things have settled down a little. How was your time in Piston County?"

"It was good. I just worked. It was a lot easier than having to deal with certain things."

"Were those things me?"

"Some of it, yes. I didn't want to hurt you, Darcy. You were going through so much, and I didn't want to have to reject you." He saw her becoming upset and reached across the table. "Don't do this. Don't pull away. You also reminded me of a lot of things I thought I had forgotten as well." He gave her hand a squeeze. "I just needed to work through them and not put myself in any position where I could hurt you."

"Do you think you'll ever be able to tell me your other things?" she asked.

"One day, maybe."

"I'd like that." He watched her cheeks heat. "I like this. You and me, being friends. I like having you as a friend, Ink."

"I like being your friend, Darcy."

She nodded. They ate their food in silence, but it wasn't uncomfortable. They were companions in this moment.

Ink was hit by guilt because he had nothing to do with this, and yet, she thought he did. He'd make it up to her in one way or another.

Chapter Eight

One month later

Living alone, for Darcy, was an incredible experience. She missed her family, of course she did, but there was something about being alone that she also loved. Her own space, her own time, and being able to just enjoy the silence.

Also, Ink was around a whole lot more. He ate meals with her and walked her to work when he was able to.

There were still obligations to The Skulls. She knew through Tabitha that they helped men, women, and children who had either been abused, hurt, or needed help after running from a sex trafficking ring.

The Skulls and Chaos Bleeds both helped another MC known as the Billionaire Bikers MC. It wasn't like the clubs she had known over the years, but something a lot bigger. It was an organization that helped others, and would use their money to intervene and to protect. They sounded amazing, and Darcy was so proud that her parents were helping others in some way.

Ink still hadn't taken his patch, even though he rode with them, worked for them, and was still very much part of the club.

"You know, you should get some wine or something," Tabitha said, rolling down the back of the sofa to sit cross-legged.

Her little friend often stayed with her on the weekends. She just couldn't say no to Tabitha.

"I don't drink, you know that."

"But where is the harm in having some?"

"One, you're underage, and so am I. If your mother even for a second suspected I was helping you break the law, you and I wouldn't be spending any time together."

"Mom wouldn't do that. She's all threat and no action most of the time."

"We're talking about your schooling here, Tabitha."

"Please, since coming here, I haven't gotten into a single fight, and I consider that a world record for me."

"You shouldn't be getting into any fights."

"I don't start them."

"You finish them?"

"Damn straight. I'm not having anyone pick on Daisy or even call out the club. I'm defending us. Anyway, topic change, have you met any cute guys?"

"It has been a month," she said.

"And, you're cute and young. Why not go on a date?"

"You have to meet people first, and between home and work, I haven't really done anything else."

Tabitha took the book out of Darcy's hand that she'd been attempting to read ever since she got home from work, only Tabitha had taken it upon herself to bug her.

"First, you need to stop sticking your head in some kind of book. It's not going to help. To date you need to get out there."

"How would you even know the first thing about dating? You've got your heart set on one guy and one guy alone."

"So? It doesn't mean I'm not an expert. I watch a lot of people, Darcy. I know what I'm talking about, and you need to trust me. Like really, really trust me." Tabitha grabbed her hands. "My mom and dad were talking about a party Saturday night at the clubhouse. They're not going. They have all kinds of people there. I think you should totally go and see what all the fuss is about."

"Tomorrow is Saturday night."

"I know."

"I thought you'd snuck in on one of these parties."

"I did, but I'm not talking about me or finding someone for me. I'm talking about you. My very best friend who I love so much and I know deserves to find love and happiness some way. Unless you've still got a thing for Ink."

"I don't have a thing for Ink."

"You're sure?"

"We're friends and we've hung out a few times, but there is nothing going on between us."

"The question is, Darcy, do you *want* there to be something going on?"

"No."

"Are you sure?"

Darcy rolled her eyes. "I'm sure. I like Ink, I do. He's a really great guy, but I'm not going to risk ruining what we have right now. I like him."

Tabitha kept staring at her.

"What?" Darcy asked.

"I'm just trying to figure out if you believe your own bullshit or if you're just trying to convince me."

"Oh, stop it." She couldn't stop laughing at her friend. "It's not bullshit. I'm happy. Besides, why would I want someone like Ink? There is a chance *it* could come back. You saw how fast he hightailed it out of there."

She noticed Tabitha got really uncomfortable all of a sudden.

"What is it? Are you worried as well?"

"It's not that. I'm just remembering what Simon once told me and what I can't tell you, and it seems so wrong to not tell you because it is really important."

"Tabitha," Darcy said.

"Oh, I can't, but I really want to."

"I thought we were friends."

"We are and this is something I shouldn't even know and I can't believe Simon told me and I've been so good up until now." Tabitha growled.

"You don't have to tell me," Darcy said.

"No, I will. It's about Ink. He didn't just leave because of you. You were a cause, but this is something else. Something big."

"It is?"

"Ink had a sister. Simon heard Devil telling Lexie. He didn't want to say anything to me, but we don't have any secrets. Not even little ones. We tell each other everything, and well, he didn't even know that Ink had a family before us."

"Wow," Darcy said. "What does his sister have to do with it?"

"She was diagnosed with cancer. It wasn't good, and she died soon after being admitted to the hospital. Haven't you noticed he rarely talks about his past, and if he does, it's always about something else?"

Darcy was taken aback. "I had no idea."

"None of us do. Apart from Devil, Lexie, Simon, and now us. No one else knows. That's his secret though. It's not just because you kind of freaked him out with your jailbait come on."

"Oh, please, asking if I was pretty is not a come on."

"If Ink had kissed you back then would you have turned him down, in all honesty?" Tabitha asked.

"No."

"I need a soda, but you see my point." Tabitha got her to feet and headed into the kitchen.

Darcy sat back, thinking about Ink, about all that

she knew about him. He was always so quiet and so private. It had been an allure of his that she liked.

"I can see that sexy look in your eye," Tabitha said. "You're totally smitten with him still, aren't you?"

"I'm not smitten. I'm just, you know, I'm fine."

"So the party tomorrow? You going?"

Darcy wrinkled her nose. "No."

"Oh, come on. It'll be fun for you to meet a guy. Please, I'll help you pick out an outfit. When are you going to start putting on weight?"

Darcy looked down at her still slender frame. During her treatment she'd lost a lot of weight, and her experience with food had been a traumatizing one. After eating she would often vomit it all back out, leaving her even more tired than when she started.

"I'm getting there." Another reason to love Tabitha, she really just spoke it like she saw it. "Hey, where are you going?"

"I'm going to pick you out a cute little outfit," Tabitha yelled from the bedroom.

Rolling her eyes, Darcy lifted herself up, putting the book on the small coffee table she'd picked up from the second hand store. It was a damn good table, and sturdy.

She found Tabitha laying out her clothing, which wasn't a lot.

Tabitha tutted. "Dresses are out the window. Skirts as well. I'm thinking some really good jeans, and this shirt." She pulled out a gypsy style white shirt with a blue print. Darcy had never worn it. "Try it on."

"Why don't I stay in? We could order takeout, watch a movie."

"No. I'm going to have to catch up with my homework and Daisy's coming for a sleepover tomorrow, so we're studying. Besides, you need a boyfriend, and I won't take no for an answer."

Darcy took the clothes from her friend and couldn't believe she was getting bossed around by a kid younger than she was.

****

Ink folded his arms as he leaned against the car. Lash was dealing with the latest woman who'd needed shelter and safety while the cops dealt with her abusive ex. That sucker was now behind bars, and Lidia could have a whole new life with her young child. When The Skulls had decided to help the law with an agreement that all of their past was laid to rest, Ink had been pessimistic. He didn't for a second think it would be this rewarding.

They had saved many men, women, and children, and each time he got to witness them finding a new life, it filled Ink with hope.

Lidia took her daughter's hand and led her into the house. She had a new identity, job, house, and a new life. The cops would keep an eye on her, and she also had a special contact number for The Skulls in case she ever needed it.

Lash slapped the hood of the car, and Ink climbed inside as his Prez got behind the wheel.

Seeing the car seat in the back, Ink grabbed it and quickly rushed it back to the woman before jogging back to the car to get gone.

"Isn't that sweet?" Lash said.

"Job well done."

"Her ex won't see the light of day. Not only did he beat the shit out of her, he also hurt the kid and has a history of violence. His chance of parole is not going to come soon, especially as he shot at a cop," Lash said. "Time to head home and party."

"You're going to the party?"

"Why not? My wife did help to organize it," Lash said. "Eva's taking care of the kids with Tiny. We want some us time. You're not coming?"

"Nah, I don't think I will."

"There's going to be some chicks available. Angel invited some people from the town."

"I think I'm going to stay home, you know. Just relax." He also intended to go see Darcy. She had been catching up on a lot of movies, and he loved sitting with her as they did. She wasn't a fan of horror, but much to his shame, he liked it when she snuggled up against him, trying to hide from the big bad wolf.

"Shame. I heard Tabitha had told Darcy about it."

Ink frowned. "Wait? What?"

"You know … Darcy. She's going to be at the party."

"She's eighteen."

"And legal. If she wants to hang out at the clubhouse she can. We can all keep an eye on her."

"This is not right," Ink said.

"Why is it not right? She's an adult now. She's got her own place, and if she wants to hang out with us, she can. Besides, any guy who hits on her will be surrounded by all of us. She's better protected at the clubhouse than she is online."

Ink ran a hand down his face, and he really couldn't believe Lash didn't have a problem with this.

"You're not serious," he said.

"Ink, I know it is hard for you to move on and all, but Darcy is growing up. She can stay and party if she wants." Lash turned on the radio. "Stop being a spoilsport. Don't you recall what it was like to be that age?"

"Yeah, and I wanted as much pussy as I could get. Darcy is not me though. She will never be me."

"I still don't see what the big deal is," Lash said.

"What if it was your daughter?" Ink asked.

"Oh, that shit isn't happening. My little girl is going to be a nun. I already see it. She won't want anything to do with boys."

"Okay, but on the off chance that she does, what then, huh? What do you suggest?" Ink asked.

"Dude, my daughter's not going down that road, okay. What is the big deal? Are you, like, jealous of her? Do you have a thing for Darcy?"

"I don't have a thing. I just care about her, and I don't want to see her get hurt."

Ink fell silent, and the only noise was coming from the radio. He didn't know why he was overreacting over this. Darcy had a right to her own life, and he couldn't recall her ever being this happy in all the time he'd known her.

The Skulls kids had been to hell and back through the club, but Darcy had to fight for something more. She'd had to fight for her life because there was nothing they could to protect her.

Running fingers through his hair, he blew out a breath, and felt … odd.

"I'm going to the party."

"Don't be a drag at the party, Ink. Let Darcy learn from her mistakes and have some fun. I'm insulted you think the club wouldn't look out for her. She's the club. Of course, we'd look out for her. She's one of us and always will be."

"I'm sorry, man. I think the time away has fucked with my head. I'm not in the right zone right now."

Lash pulled up outside Ink's building. "You're coming to the clubhouse tonight?"

"Yeah, I'm coming. I wouldn't miss it."

"You know that leather cut is waiting for you."

"I haven't earned it."

"If you'd turned your back on the club, run away and not had anything to do with us, I wouldn't give it you back. You didn't do that. Whenever I needed you over the past three years, you came running. You were still part of the club, but I get it. You think none of us has needed a break, some down time? You're wrong. We've all needed it, some more than others. I'm not going to hold that against you. Besides, you also helped Devil, and anything that can bring our clubs together, I'm all about."

Ink nodded. "I'll think about it."

"You do that."

Lash had to have the last word.

Climbing out of the car, Ink didn't linger to chat. He merely made his way up to his place, only to stop with the key in the lock.

Glancing to the elevator, he instead took off, heading to Darcy's place. Knocking on her door, he waited for a response, only for nothing to come. He knocked again, and of course, there was no answer because she wasn't there, she was at the damn party.

He shouldn't care.

Darcy was her own person, and she knew how to take care of herself. But he couldn't let it go.

Rushing back to his own apartment, he took a quick shower to wash off the day, and got ready as fast as he could. He wasn't going to let anyone hurt Darcy, and he would always be there for her.

Chapter Nine

Sitting at the corner of the bar, Darcy nursed her soda and watched everyone. She'd spent a great deal of time at the club, and for the most part, it had all been rather tame. Some of what she was seeing was not tame.

There were no kids around, and it would seem the parents liked to play. When she saw Lacey and Whizz making out in a booth, she had no choice but to avert her gaze. Maybe mixing kids and parents wasn't such a good idea. Her own parents weren't here. Michael was though, and seeing him walk around as if he owned the place pissed her off.

She knew from Tabitha that the younger girl had in fact cut Michael for some kind of infraction. Being in the hospital she'd not gotten the full story, and Tabitha had been vague about it.

"The point of going to a party is to actually enjoy it," Drew said, taking a seat beside her.

"Are you kidding? I'm having so much fun. I'm drinking and staring at the bar because it is the only safe place to look. I think they're trying to melt my eyeballs forever," she said.

Drew laughed. "It takes some getting used to. It has been a long time since a party like this was thrown. What made you come in the first place?"

"Tabitha. She thinks I need to start meeting people. Guys to be more specific."

"The girl that's taken is offering you out to the world."

"It's not like that." She felt a need to defend her friend.

"I know it's not. It's good to see you out. How is work and life and stuff?"

"Oh, it's all good. You know. Busy. I like to keep

busy though. It takes my mind off everything else." She shrugged. "How about you? Have you met any hot girl yet? You got any girl hot and bothered?" She cringed. "I have no idea what I'm talking about or even why I'm talking like this." Drew was laughing, so she considered that a plus.

"I get it, and no. No one for me."

"Have you dated a lot?"

"Not really. Dating is not on my list of things to do right now." Drew looked across the room, and Darcy followed his gaze seeing Steven and Sally together.

"You got a thing for her still?"

"No. I just like to see her happy, you know."

"I doubt she wanted to hurt you."

"Sally doesn't have a nasty bone in her body. She never told me there was a single chance with me. I know that."

"Then why are you still looking at her like you got a chance?" Darcy asked.

Drew sighed. "I'm not. I'm trying not to."

"You do want her though," Darcy said.

"I'm fine."

"It has been years." She lifted up in her chair. "And you're not going to be miserable anymore."

"Darcy?"

"Nope, don't even start with me. We're going to find you a date, and you're going to go on it."

"I'm older than you. I can find someone to date," he said.

"I know you *can*, but the point is, you haven't. You're living in the idea that Sally is going to come to you. She's not, and I'm not trying to be cruel." She'd read enough books to know that the Sally and Stevens of the world stayed together.

She had been rooting for the couple for as long as

she could remember. With her stupid crush on Ink, it had given her hope that one day he'd look at her like she was more than just a kid, or Emily and Blaine's kid.

She needed to learn to move on as well, and to stop dwelling in the past. Ink would never see her as something more, and she really wanted to find that special someone. Even though, deep in her heart, she had a feeling Ink was her special someone, Ink didn't feel the same way about her.

"What about her, the blonde?" she asked.

The moment she pointed the other woman out, there was a huge high-pitched laugh that made her wince it was so loud.

"Yep, scrap that." She looked around the room, and when she saw her target, a brunette with a sweet smile who also looked a little out of place, she didn't give Drew a chance to tell her no.

Rushing over to the woman just as Adam approached, she looked at the British Skull and shook her head.

"Are you calling dibs on the brown head?" he asked.

"Yes."

"You're a lesbian."

"Adam, there are lot of other women in this club tonight. You can have your pick of any number of them."

"I want this one."

"Tough. This one is mine." She nudged Adam back. "Hey, my name's Darcy. I don't think I've ever seen you at the club before." She held her hand out.

"Hi, no, this is my first time."

"I didn't catch your name," Darcy said.

"It's Jade."

"Hey, Jade. It's good to see you."

"Do you come here often?" Jade asked.

"Well, erm, my parents are actually members of the club, so I'm here a lot."

"Oh, they don't mind you hanging out, partying?"

"They don't seem to, no." This couldn't get any more awkward. "How about we go and have a drink? How about that?"

She grabbed Jade's hand and led her back to her part of the bar.

Drew was glaring at her, and she forced a smile to her lips.

"Hey, Drew, this is Jade. Jade, this is my good friend, Drew. He's an actual member of the club, unlike me." Darcy grabbed a stool, drawing it closer so Jade could sit between them.

"It's nice to meet you, Jade," Drew said.

"And you. My friend said this was the best place to come on a Saturday night," Jade said.

"Where's your friend?" Drew asked.

"She left with someone."

Darcy pressed her lips together, to keep her opinion on friends who abandoned others to a minimum. She ordered them a round of drinks, staying completely soda for herself, while buying shots for her friends.

The music began to get loud, and she encouraged both Jade and Drew to head out onto the dance floor to enjoy a dance.

She was watching them, admiring all the couples that chose to dance. Angel and Lash were wrapped around each other. Killer and Kelsey. Zero and Prudence.

Taking a deep breath, she felt tears fill her eyes. There was a chance she wouldn't have gotten to see this, to watch her family together.

She had tried to keep a distance from all of them. Each day she had, she had cherished more than the last. Being on the children's ward, she had made so many friends, and with them, she had seen life and death. Wiping a tear, she turned to face the bar, drinking her soda.

She shouldn't have come to the bar. This place wasn't for her. Just as she was about to leave, someone sat down beside her.

"I didn't think I'd see you at a Skulls party."

Ink was dressed in jeans and a shirt. His heavily inked arms were on full display in a white shirt that didn't hide his very sexy and handsome body.

"Ink," she said.

"Are you enjoying the party?" he asked.

"Yeah, I am." She nodded toward the dance floor. "Look what I just made happen."

"Drew with a chick?"

"Yep."

"About time."

"I totally agree."

"You're not here to find someone for yourself?"

Her cheeks heated, and she thought about Tabitha. "Yes, but that's not going to happen. I'm going to head home, actually. I'm tired. It has been a long day." She didn't think it was a total waste coming here because one look at Drew, and she knew she'd made the right decision.

"Before you go, dance with me."

"Why?"

"Every woman should have a dance before leaving a party. Come on." He took hold of her hand, and she didn't fight him.

The crush she had on Ink wasn't gone.

Each time he was with her, every single touch and caress, it seemed to blister her body with a need. The heat from his hands in her body made her ache in ways she had never known before.

What had started out as a crush certainly hadn't ended like one.

She followed him onto the dance floor, and as he pulled her in close with his hands on the base of her back, she kept trying to focus on anything that wasn't his face or his mouth. His lips looked so tempting, and she wondered what they would be like to kiss, to press her lips against his.

"You look really pretty tonight."

"Thank you. Tabitha dressed me." She closed her eyes. "She picked out my clothes."

He laughed. "I know what you mean. Do you like the party?" he asked.

"It's good. Tabitha wants me to start dating, and the only way to do that is to go out in the world and meet people."

"What do you want to do?" he asked.

She thought about it while staring at his neck. Why did it look so good that she wanted to kiss it? *Get your head out of the clouds, Darcy.* "I want to date. I do want to meet someone. I feel I've missed so much of my life already, and I don't want to miss anymore. What about you? Are you going to date?"

"No, I don't date. You're not going to meet the person for you here, Darcy."

"You don't know that."

"I know enough to know you're better than this."

She sighed. "I think it's time for me to go home."

She pulled away from him, and fortunately he didn't put up a fight.

****

Ink nearly hit his head on the underside of a car when someone slammed something hard down on the hood.

"What the fuck?" He pulled himself out from

under the car, and sure enough, there was Tabitha, glaring at him, looking pissy. Her long, blonde hair looked like a wild mess. "What do you want, Tabitha?"

"Not only will you not date Darcy but you then get in the way of her finding someone."

He should have known Tabitha would find out. After walking Darcy home from the party, she hadn't talked to him. That had been a week and a half ago, and he didn't like the silence that was happening between them. He liked listening to her talk.

"You should be in school."

"I got half a day, and I figured I'd come and deal with you."

"You're a kid."

"Can't you deal with the fact Darcy wants someone else that is not you?" Tabitha had her hands on her hips and was glaring at him.

He wiped his hands on the cloth and stared right at her. Tabitha didn't scare him. "She wasn't going to find a guy at the clubhouse. Not one worth her time."

"You know who is worth her time?"

Ink stayed silent.

"Whatever game it is you're playing, it's not going to work," Tabitha said.

"Darcy will find the right guy when she's ready."

"I know. We went out for coffee the other day, and a nice guy named Ward asked her out." Tabitha looked down at her wrist. "I think they'll be enjoying their lunch date right about now."

"Where?" Ink asked.

"Where else would a hot date go down while Darcy is working? They're having a picnic near the library. Now, for someone who doesn't care, you don't look impressed." She folded her arms, looking a little too cocky for his liking.

"I'm out of here," Ink said.

"Oh, Ink, Ward is certainly no member of the club." Tabitha winked at him. "She's perfectly safe."

Grabbing his keys, he took off out of the clubhouse without saying a word to anyone. Tabitha was turning into a meddling bitch, and he didn't like that. It reminded him of Tate, and he knew she could be a problem. The ride to the library didn't take him long. He parked his bike and rushed out behind a small toilet building only to stop. The library was near a large picnic field where a lot of couples had dates and ate lunch.

He saw Darcy clearly.

The guy she was with wasn't someone he recognized. Whatever he'd said to Darcy had made her laugh though. Her head was thrown back, and she looked so incredibly happy. He stopped, watching her. She looked happy. She'd pinned her short locks up, and she wore a pair of jeans and a large shirt.

This Ward was making her laugh, and giving her happiness, and it bothered him. He'd never been like this with anyone else, so seeing her like this, happy, it was hard for him to go and interrupt.

You're also jealous.

He remembered how she'd try to make him laugh or talk to him. When she had a crush on him, she'd always tried to make him happy.

This Ward, he didn't know who the guy was, but he wasn't going to let Darcy get hurt.

He stepped around the building and walked with purpose toward them. Darcy saw him first, and the smile on her lips vanished. Now that hurt. He'd done nothing to hurt her in all the time he'd known her.

"Ink," she said.

"Darcy, if I knew you needed to have lunch brought to you, I'd have dealt with it." He was being a grade-A dick, but once he started, he couldn't seem to stop.

"Is this a friend of yours?" Ward the prick asked.

"Yes. He's friends with my mom and dad."

He clenched his teeth together, hating that she'd made that distinction between them. She'd never once referred to him as her parents' friend.

"Lunch is pretty much finished, and I think I should start heading back. It has been a pleasure, Darcy. We must do this again sometime."

"You have my number."

Now Ink wanted to destroy the bastard's phone. Was he the only one that cared about her safety? Right now, it fucking felt like it, and it was pissing him off.

The picnic table was wrapped up, and he reached for Darcy.

"She'll call you when she wants to see you again."

Ward didn't take a hint and leaned in, kissing her cheek.

Ink wanted to hurt that pretty face. To mark it up so the fucker knew never to touch her again.

Finally, Ward left, and he and Darcy were alone.

"What the hell?" Darcy asked. "What was that?"

"What do you even know about that guy?"

"How did you know I was even here on a date?" she asked. She stared at him and laughed. "Wow, Tabitha. She was the one who encouraged me to go on this date, and yet she's telling you all about it."

"She should tell me, especially when you put your life in danger."

"Danger? There was no danger. I didn't go back to his place, nor did I go somewhere in his car. I had a picnic lunch with him close to where I work, surrounded by people. I'm not stupid, Ink. I know what I'm doing!"

She yelled at him.

"You're so determined to date. That guy could be a serial killer. You ever thought of that?"

She gasped. "So you're saying the only kind of guy I could possibly get is the kind that goes around killing people. There is nothing wrong with wanting to date. It's a perfectly logical thing to want to do. I don't want to be alone and miserable for the rest of my life."

"Guys are not just going to want to date, Darcy. They're going to want a whole lot of other things."

"I know, and I want them too."

"You want sex."

"Yes!" She yelled, getting into his face. "I want to experience *everything*. Do you want me to spell it out for you, Ink? I want everything. I want sex. I want to be desired, needed, craved, loved. You name it, I want it all, and it has to start with dating. With finding a guy who is not afraid of the club or my family." She shoved him hard. "Now leave me alone."

****

"You know, meddling is not a good thing," Tate said, stepping into the mechanic shop.

Tabitha held a spanner in her hands and turned to look at her older sister. They had different moms, but as far as she was concerned, they were true sisters. "I think meddling is good. If it achieves the same outcome."

"And you think getting between Ink and Darcy is a good thing?" Tate asked, arms folded.

Tabitha sighed. "Are you going to give me the third degree here?"

"No. I want to make sure you know what you're doing."

"I know what I'm doing."

"You do?"

"Darcy is in love with Ink, and if he gives it a

shot, I think Ink has a thing for Darcy. Let's face it, you don't go rushing out for no reason." Tabitha shoved some gum in her mouth. "Besides, Ward looked like a total asshole."

"He did?"

"Yep. He thought a cheap-ass mocha latte was all it took to get a girl's number."

"It did work," Tate said.

"No, it didn't. I meddled a little. Darcy didn't want to give him her number, but I made her concede because I knew this would happen. There's no way Darcy would go somewhere private to have lunch with a stranger. This was perfect and planned." Tabitha jumped up on the table, crossed her legs and smiled at her sister.

"I think I've made a monster out of you," Tate said.

"And you look really impressed with that."

"I fear for your enemies, Tab. You keep up this attitude, and no one will ever take you on."

Chapter Ten

"Darcy, come on, I know you're in there. I saw you come home, remember," Ink said.

Darcy stood right by her door with Ink knocking on the wood. She had only just arrived home, and she'd put another homemade pasta bake into the oven. Angel had showed her how to get ahead on a Sunday so she could spend more time enjoying the week without having to constantly wonder what was for dinner.

She didn't want to open the door.

She was still so incredibly mad at Ink. Not only had she admitted what she wanted to him, but there had been witnesses to her anger, and she was mortified. What if her parents found out?

"I don't think it's a good idea you visiting me, Ink. The point of me being alone is to, you know, be alone."

"Don't do this. I said some stupid things, and I want to talk to you. Not through a door and not for everyone to hear. Please, Darcy, let me apologize."

He sounded so genuine. She closed her eyes, resting her head against the door.

Open it up for him.

Don't be a pain.

Just ... talk to him.

Tucking her hair behind her ears, she opened the door, and there he stood. His hands rested either side of the doorframe, and he looked so good, even with the sad look in his eyes.

"Hey," she said.

"I'm so sorry."

"It's fine."

She left the door open, turning back into her place and taking a seat on the sofa. She crossed her legs and watched him as he closed the door and moved toward her.

Even mad at him, she wanted him, and that's what was making it hard to respond to Ward's text. Tabitha helped to set the date up, but nothing else.

"You're mad?" he asked.

"I'm not mad. I don't know what I am to be honest. I'm just trying to figure everything out, you know. I'm not meaning to be a bitch or anything." She blew out a breath.

"Did you like this guy?" Ink asked.

"I don't know. He seemed like a nice guy, and that's the kind of guy I should be going for. Ugh! This is so insane. I'm sorry." She pressed her hands against her face, rubbing to try to clear the fog from her mind.

This crush had to stop. She needed to move on with her life.

"You'll find someone," he said.

"Yeah, because a guy is totally out there."

"You're a good person, Darcy. Any man would be lucky to have you."

She nibbled her lip, trying not to look at him.

"What is it?" he asked.

She tilted her head, looking at him. "I think I'm being delusional."

"Why?"

"Look at me. I can't have kids. The chances of me being able to conceive are incredibly low. There's still a chance I could end up back in the hospital. I can't do that to anyone. I don't want to do that." She shook her head, not wanting to bring up too much for fear of hurting Ink. "I think it's best to be alone."

"You'll never be alone," Ink said. "You'll always have me."

She forced a smile to her lips. "Thank you." She

leaned her head back against the sofa.

"Also, the right guy will come your way, Darcy. You just got to believe it." He took hold of her hand, and her heart raced as he pressed a kiss to her knuckles. "I know there is a person in this world for everyone."

She smiled and quickly withdrew her hand. "I better check on dinner. Do you want to stay for dinner?"

"I'd love to."

When she got to her feet, her cell phone buzzed in her back pocket, and she pulled it out to see another invitation from Ward. The guy didn't know when to stop.

She should be feeling flattered he wanted anything to do with her, but in all honesty, she was exhausted.

Dating sounded great, but the truth was, she just wanted the time to live her life. To go to parties, and one day get blind drunk so her father had to carry her home. Hang out with friends that were older than she was, rather than younger.

Deleting Ward's number, she smiled. She could do this without finding a guy. Grabbing the food out of the oven, she saw it was cooked, and served both her and Ink up a plate. She took out two beers, which her dad had dropped by, and made her way back into the sitting room. She didn't imagine her father expected her to give the beers to Ink.

"Here you go," she said.

"You bought beer."

"My dad bought beer. How about that?" She winked at him. "Beer and food. To new beginnings and leaving the past behind." She held out her bottle, and Ink clicked his bottle with hers.

"To finding our soulmates."

****

One year later

"You really need to cover your eyes," Ink said, his hands poised over Darcy's face.

"You know this is kidnapping, right? You took me from the library, dragged me to the middle of nowhere, and now you take away my ability to see. This is so not fair."

"Life isn't fair, sweetheart," he said. "I told you not to be worried or afraid. This is your birthday present."

"Oh, yay, my birthday present, what fun. Please, can we stop this now? My birthday was a couple of months ago, and if my memory serves me right, you were the only one not to give me a present."

"I forgot."

"Exactly, so can we please go? I don't need presents," she said.

Ink wasn't going to take no for an answer. He'd planned this for the past week. Darcy never got to go camping, and as a result it was something that was always promised to her, but she never got a chance to do. Blaine and Emily weren't keen on the idea of going camping, and none of the other Skull kids wanted to go, so he decided to go ahead and give her this experience.

"Why do I feel like I'm in the woods?" she asked.

"Because you are in the woods."

"Are you going to kill me?"

"If I was going to kill you, I would have done it already."

"Ugh, this is so not how I imagined spending my Friday night."

"Did you have a hot date?" he asked. It had been a long time since Darcy went on any date, and he knew because he'd kept an eye on her.

Seeing her with that guy at the picnic nearly a year ago, he'd not wanted to deal with his feelings of her being with anyone else. He'd never been a possessive kind of guy, so this was all new to him.

"Hot date? Please, this is me. I don't believe in hot dates. Just disappointments."

All of Darcy's dates had been with him. They'd attended parties together, gone to the fair, and they'd even gone to the movies together. Darcy was a cool person to hang out with, and he loved her company.

Once he saw the camp up ahead, he heard her sniff the air.

"Are you going to set me on fire? I'm not a witch."

"Come on, stop being an ass," he said. He walked her up to the campsite, and when he was sure everything was fine, he lowered his hands. "Surprise." He stepped to one side so he could watch her reaction.

She looked shocked. "Camping."

"Yes. You mentioned how you'd never done it."

"Oh," she said. "This is the big surprise?"

"Yes."

There was a pause. "Great. Who is joining us?"

"Erm, no one. No one else wanted to join, so it's just me and you. I got us some marshmallows and a hot dog."

"We're camping in the middle of the woods alone."

"Yep, that about sums it up."

"Right," she said. "And you think this is a pretty good birthday present? Sorry, sorry, late birthday present."

"I think it's pretty special, yeah."

"Oh," she said. "Such fun." She pressed her lips together.

"I'm sensing a theme here."

"Ink, I hate to break it to you, but there's a pretty

good reason I've never gone camping," she said.

"You don't like it? You loved sitting in trees."

"Yeah, because I could climb down and use a normal bathroom. I'm not spending days at a time in the middle of nowhere. I hate it," she said. "It's the outdoors, and it's cold and miserable, and wet. What about coyotes? What about wolves? Ugh, we're going to die. I have just stepped into my own horror movie, and we're all going to die."

Ink pulled her into his arms. "You're not going to die. I'm sorry. I thought you'd really enjoy this. It's me and you, a fire, food. It could be fun."

In the past year he'd earned his cut back with his work with The Skulls, not that he had needed to. The Skulls knew why he'd left, and the patch was still his to take when he wanted it. For Ink, *he* felt like he had to earn it back. The best part of the past year was spending as much time as he could with Darcy. She was an incredible woman. Her passion, her fire, it was amazing to witness, and when she entered a room, he was drawn to her. She was in his thoughts constantly. He had also come clean to the club about his sister. The club knew he'd walked away because of Darcy's interest in him. He was no longer keeping his sister a secret from the club, and had come clean. He hadn't told Darcy the truth in person yet, but he wanted to when the moment was right. At first it was to make it up to her for leaving, but then that had all changed. He loved her company and enjoyed watching her as she flourished away from her parents. She loved her job and her apartment, which hadn't taken her long to make it her own. "Will you at least give it a chance?"

"Sure." She snuggled into her coat. "Show me everything."

He held her hand and took her to their camping

tent. There were two beds in there, and he'd only gotten them one tent big enough for the two of them.

"Oh, wow," she said. "Why are we sharing?"

"I figured it would be safer. You know, in case of wolves or coyotes and stuff."

"You've got what it takes to take on those kinds of dangerous animals?" she asked.

"I can protect you, Darcy. Make no mistake about that." He moved back toward the small fire and dropped down a cushion. "Take a seat."

"I'm seeing a certain excitement here. You love doing this, don't you? Camping."

"I don't mind getting back to nature. There are a lot of other things that people can do, but this is all about nature. Come on, sit."

She lowered herself down onto the cushion, and he grabbed himself one, sitting with her. Next, he sorted them both out some hot dogs from his little bag of tricks.

"Did Angel go shopping for all of this?" she asked.

"Yep, and she prepared us a thermos of her finest cocoa, but I also brought something to help keep the cold away." He held up a bottle of really good scotch, and she laughed.

"You know I don't drink."

"I know, which is why the cocoa is there."

"One sip shouldn't hurt."

He winked at her. "That, miss, you are right about. No harm ever came from just one sip."

They roasted the hot dogs, and Ink did his best to toast the buns. He'd also brought some condiments for the hot dogs, and he held them open while Darcy made up their food.

As he took a large bite, ketchup and mustard squirted out of the side of his, hitting him in the corner of the mouth.

He didn't mind as Darcy kept on giggling. It was a good sound for her, one he loved hearing.

They ate another hot dog each and moved on to the marshmallows. He asked her about work, and as usual, she began to tell him all the latest gossip within the town. Most of it he didn't care for, and some of it was just plain out soap opera material. For him, he got to hear Darcy talk, and that was the whole point of it.

"Besides, enough about me. Tell me what is going on with you."

"Not a whole lot. We haven't been called upon by Michael Granito or the Billionaire Bikers, so it has been a quiet couple of weeks. I've been helping out at the gym. I tend to move equipment around, and wherever they need muscle, that's pretty much where I am."

"I do love that you finally took your leather cut back," she said, touching his arm. "It suits you."

Ink didn't like how nice it was to have her hands on him. He'd noticed over the past year each time they hung out, it was getting harder and harder to deny his attraction to her, which made this all incredibly dangerous.

Darcy removed her hand, and he watched her as she began to eat her warm, gooey marshmallow.

"This is really good." Her tongue played across the sticky mess, and it got on her fingers.

His dick hardened, and he sat up, blowing out the fire on his own and removing the scorched skin.

Get your fucking head in the game, Ink.

This wasn't supposed to be some kind of romantic getaway or even anything that reminded him she was a woman. A woman that in the last year had filled out as well. She'd been able to put on some of the weight she'd lost, and she looked incredible. Her body had filled out, and he even recalled when she realized she had breasts.

She'd showed him. Not her naked tits, but the fact the dress she wore only served to enhance her cleavage. She had also done a little jump up and down dance that made them wiggle.

That's the kind of friend he'd become to her, the one she could talk about anything and show her body off to.

All the time, he was having a hard time dealing with these new feelings. Darcy wasn't a child anymore, and it was growing abundantly clear that she was in fact a woman, and soon that woman would have wants. His only problem was she didn't show any signs as seeing him as the kind of person to give her those wants. The crush she once had on him was long gone, and in its place, he'd been sidelined to friend.

"I can't believe how messy I still get eating these."

He handed her some sanitary wipes, which Angel had remembered to purchase. He wouldn't have even thought of it.

"You want another marshmallow?" he asked.

"Nah, I'm full. What I'd like to try though, is that sip."

"You want a sip?"

"Hell, yeah, I'm camping. I'm going to make the memory of it worthwhile."

He finished his marshmallow and poured them both a large drink.

Handing a cup to Darcy, he watched as she sniffed the air and wrinkled her nose.

"Just give it a try. One tiny sip, remember that."

"One little sip." She pressed the cup to her mouth and took one.

INK

He expected the coughing, but what he didn't was her to keep on taking another sip.

Chapter Eleven

Darcy finished off her first cup of scotch, and she felt fine. Her arms and body felt a little weird, but it was a good kind of weird. Like she was floating a little, or swimming without any water.

She watched as Ink drank a whole glass and poured himself another.

"I'll take another."

"I don't think you should."

"Come on. I'm camping. I'm out in the great outdoors, and may I add, I never for a second thought I'd ever come here."

"You didn't."

"Nope. Please, let me have another."

"Fine. Fine." He poured her another cup full, and she sipped it down. The buzz was only getting better and she quickly gulped it down, but Ink refused to fill her another cup. She rested her head on his shoulder.

"You know, Ink, I had the biggest crush on you growing up."

"I know."

She giggled. "I think everyone knew, and I was under this big whole illusion that I could keep it a secret." She snorted as she giggled. "Everyone knew, and they all knew that you'd ran away from me because I couldn't keep my big old mouth shut." She slapped a hand across her face. "Sorry, I shouldn't say anything, should I?"

He laughed. "Someone is a little drunk."

"Is this what drunk feels like? No wonder my dad used to drink so much." She got to her feet, and Ink took hold of her hand. "I feel incredible, and I feel like dancing. Doing a whole lot of dancing." She swayed her body with Ink still holding her. She felt completely fluid, like nothing and no one could ever harm her. "I don't want this to stop."

"Oh, believe me, not only will it stop, but you're going to crash big time."

"I don't care. I love this. Oh wow, I totally love this. Whoop-whoop." Her voice echoed into the night, and Ink finally stood with her and they danced to some imaginary music, and it all was amazing.

When he sat down, Darcy knew she wouldn't be able to do this again. This had to be something she did right now, without any witnesses, with no way of him ever escaping.

She straddled his lap, and she felt something hard digging against her, but didn't think much of it.

"Darcy?" His hands were on her back, and even through the jacket she wore, she knew he was holding it and to her, it was the best feeling in the world.

"I'm going to tell you something, and I don't want you to freak out or run away." She kissed his cheek, and he tensed beneath her. "My crush on you never disappeared. It never went away. You think I deleted Ward's number because I wanted to live my life, but you're wrong. I deleted his number because I got tired of pretending there was someone else I wanted when in fact, all I wanted was you." She cupped his face. "Please don't run away. I'm not underage. I'm not trying to trap you. I get it if you stop being my friend. I love you, Ink. I've loved you for a really long time, and I'm going to keep on loving you until the day I die."

"Darcy."

She slammed her lips down on his, holding his face as she kissed him. His lips were firm and unyielding. When she was about to pull away, Ink stopped her. One of his hands moved up from her back to sink his fingers into her hair, holding her firmly against him. She slid her tongue across his lips, and when he opened his mouth, she plunged inside, tasting him. She released a little moan and wanted nothing more than to be completely owned by him.

"Darcy?" he said, breaking from the kiss as she moved to his neck.

"Please don't push me away."

"I won't. But this is not the time."

"Why?"

"Because, you're drunk. When we do this, I want you to remember everything."

"I will remember this."

"This is the first time you've drunk a whole lot of scotch."

She rubbed herself against him, feeling how wet she was. Her clit pulsed as she pressed it against the denim of her jeans.

They both groaned, and the other hand at her back moved down to squeeze her ass. She whimpered his name, but he didn't stop there. He tugged on her hair, drawing her head back so that he could kiss and lick across her heated flesh. Her neck had never felt so good, and with his mouth on her, she didn't want him to stop.

With her eyes closed, she ground down on his dick, and she suddenly realized he was hard. Ink was hard for her. He wanted her, and she couldn't see a problem for them to be together.

Not anymore.

"Please," she said.

He growled. "Not now." He pulled away. "What the fuck do you do to me, Darcy?"

"I make you want me."

"Yes, but I didn't bring you here to have sex."

"I don't mind. You'll be my first, Ink. Please, I never stopped wanting you. I've never been able to stop wanting you. My crush never disappeared." She smiled. "I still have a crush on you, Ink, and I want you to be my first."

"The first time we're together, it's going to be with you remembering all of it," he said.

She pouted.

"Don't give me that face. I know what I'm talking about." He kissed her again. "Come on, the sun is down."

She glanced around the campfire, and sure enough, the sun was down, and it had gotten dark during her drinking and making out.

"Do you want to go and get me naked?" she asked.

"Darcy, I packed a pair of pajamas for you. They're in the tent. Go and put them on."

"Don't you want to see me naked?"

He cupped her face. "More than anything, and I shouldn't. This wasn't supposed to be about that."

"Plans change. We all change." She wasn't going to let Ink know how she felt, and yet, look at how that had turned out. At the first opportunity, she had told him that not only did she still have a crush but she wanted him.

Her body was on fire with need for him, and it wasn't going to go away, not easily. Ink helped her off his lap and walked her toward the tent. "You don't want to watch me?"

"I'm being a gentleman here, Darcy."

"I didn't think bikers had it in them to be a gentleman."

"You bring it out in me."

"Then I command you to put that gentleman away, and focus on me." She stepped toward him, but he caught her hands. "You're being a spoilsport."

"In the morning, if you remember this and feel the same way, we'll talk. Until then, get changed."

"I thought camping was supposed to be fun."

"It is, and it will be. Next time I won't bring the scotch."

"At least you know there is totally going to be a next time." She entered the tent, and sure enough, some of her pajamas were resting on the end of the sleeping bags. It took her several attempts to get out of her clothes, and all too soon, her body started to feel sleepy.

Opening the tent, she showed him she was indeed dressed and yawned.

"I think it's time for someone to go to bed," he said.

"Join me, Ink."

He helped her down into the covers and stroked her hair. "I'll be there in a minute."

She didn't remember him getting into bed as she passed out within a couple of minutes of her head hitting the pillow.

****

The following morning, Ink held back Darcy's hair as she vomited near one of the fallen trees. He had an arm banded around her waist, keeping her upright. He pulled her hair off her face as she kept on throwing up.

"I'm never drinking again."

"It's why a lot of people vow not to do it."

"But it felt so good, and now it's just so awful."

Ink didn't want to get his hopes up that even for a second that she remembered last night. With Darcy, he'd promised himself he wouldn't be selfish with her, even though every single part of him wanted to. He wanted her to fall in love with him. She had admitted to a crush, but he wanted so much more from her.

"Please make it stop."

"It will."

She finally stopped, and he handed her some water for her to gargle with, and then some mouthwash.

Once she was done, he picked her up and carried her back to their tent, easing her back into the sleeping bag.

"Don't go," she said, when he made to step out.

"I'm going to make us both some coffee."

"Okay, but don't go."

He leaned down, kissing the top of her head. "I won't leave you."

He left the tent and got to work boiling some water with a pot over the fire he built. He hoped Darcy would sleep a little before the coffee was ready and help ease any headache she might have.

Humming to himself, he tried to keep his mind on the coffee and not on how good it felt to have Darcy on his lap, grinding against his dick like she had last night. He'd not brought her here to fuck; he meant that. They were together because they both wanted to be.

She wasn't dating anyone, and neither was he.

The only person he truly wanted—and the person he'd denied himself—was Darcy.

"Get your fucking head in the game, Ink."

The water boiled, after what seemed like a lifetime. He made them both black coffees, carrying the mugs back into the tent. Darcy was lying there, eyes open, and she smiled at him.

"I like it when you hum," she said. "You've got a nice voice."

"You're the first person to tell me that, and I know you're lying."

"I don't mind hearing it. You sounded happy."

"That's because I am happy."

"You are?" she asked.

"I am."

He sat down on the sleeping bag and handed her a cup. She sat up, leaning her back against the tent a little as she took it.

"How are you feeling?"

"My insides feel like they've been burned, my head is exploding, and I also remember everything about last night."

He sipped at his coffee, waiting for her to explain more.

"I hope I didn't embarrass you last night."

"You could never embarrass me. It's not possible."

She frowned. "I remember a lot about last night. About how I told you the truth of my feelings. I told you I loved you, but I also recall you didn't rebuff me. You didn't tell me no or ask me to leave."

"I know."

"Why? That's what I don't get. You ran while we were in the hospital, and now you're not running."

He stared down into his cup, knowing deep in his heart this moment would come. "Because I'm not afraid."

"You're not?"

"No. You were young, Darcy, but it wasn't just your question or behavior that made me run." So he told her exactly why he ran. He talked about his sister and what he'd lost, and how she'd wanted him to be a knight in shining armor but he couldn't save her. The guilt and the overwhelming loss. Then he told her his fears of rejecting her and what it would mean for her. "I couldn't do that to you. I couldn't help, no matter how much I wanted to. Believe me, I did. I want to help you all the time, but I can't do it. I'm not a hero. You were way too young. I could have gone to prison. You will always be beautiful, but you were fifteen, going through something that no person should ever have to go through."

Darcy grabbed his hand and cupped his face. "I wish I could take back what I did. What I said. I remember that day so clearly. I was so … afraid. My feelings for you had only gotten stronger, and there I was, with cancer, hearing all the crazy statistics of what could happen. I didn't want to die, and I didn't want to not ever get the chance to kiss you. I was completely wrong in putting you in that position, and I am so sorry for what I did. You *are* a hero, Ink. You're not a doctor. You can only do so much, but look at what you've done with The Skulls. You're a hero."

"I'm not. I'm a guy that does the right thing."

She sighed. "But not every guy would do it. Some would look the other way. I've seen the damage that some men do to women. They … abuse them. They steal their trust and shatter it. I see that in them, and I know for a fact you would never, ever do something like that. You're a hero, but like most heroes, you refuse to see it." She took his hand. "I hope one day you'll be able to see yourself the way I do."

He squeezed her hand. "I won't push you away."

"You didn't want things to go further."

"In drink, we do crazy things."

"You weren't drunk, and you kissed me back."

"Because I wanted to, Darcy. Drink didn't make me do anything last night. That was all me."

"So you're saying…"

"I'm saying that I wanted to kiss you last night. I wanted your lips on mine. I wanted it all, but I'm not going to take something that you're not going to freely give me." He glanced around their tent. "I'm also not going to do it while we're on a camping trip." He saw her cheeks redden. "What are you thinking?"

"We could head home. I'm not big on the whole camping thing. This has been my favorite time, but we could go back to my place or your place and pick up this conversation."

"If I get you to a room, Darcy, you won't remain a virgin for long."

He saw her smile. "That's what I'm hoping for."

"Do you want me to take your virginity?"

"Ink, I've been wanting you to take my virginity for a hell of a lot longer than sipping at a bottle of scotch."

****

"You are aware that the more times you throw Ink and Darcy together, the bigger the chance is they're going to end up together," Angel said.

Blaine and Emily shared a look, and Angel looked toward Lash.

"You want them to end up together?" Lash asked.

Instead of going camping, Lash had insisted they invite Emily and Blaine over for dinner. She knew when her husband made suggestions like that, it was because he wanted some information and was using her parties to get what he wanted.

"Darcy has always had a crush on Ink," Emily said.

"She's not a little girl anymore," Angel said. "Those crushes can explode and mean a lot more."

"We know, and we also know that Ink in his way cares for her. After everything that has happened with Darcy, nearly losing her, we don't want her to go through life never knowing that love and happiness is out there," Emily said.

"I agreed to not give Ink shit if my girl ends up with him. There's an age gap there, and yes, I don't exactly like it, but I've got no choice, do I? I've got to see this through. She's my little girl. She will always be my little girl, but I don't want her to have a half-life. If all she needs to be happy is that six foot fucking tattooed asshole, it's what she'll get. I'll be happy for her."

"And that's why you encouraged Ink to take her camping," Lash said.

"Oh, no. I'm not going to make it entirely easy for him. Darcy hates fucking camping even more than I do. He's going to have to work at getting my daughter's heart," Blaine said.

Angel smiled. She'd been the one to pack their lunch, and she knew Darcy. She had seen the way Darcy had looked at Ink, and knew this wasn't going to be a battle of wills. Darcy loved Ink, and if she wasn't mistaken, Ink loved Darcy. The two just didn't realize it yet, but she hoped after their trip, they would.

Chapter Twelve

Darcy ran to her bathroom, pulling off her clothes and climbing in the shower. Not only was she trying to rush, but she also had to be careful not to injure herself, which she nearly did, sliding across the bathroom floor in socks.

Growing up and wanting to go out, she had mastered the quick shower, which she did right now.

The moment the conditioner was out of her hair, the water was off, and she wrung out her hair in the hope that she would help it dry quickly. Wrapping a towel around her body, she did the same to her hair and rushed to her bedroom.

When she opened her wardrobe, there wasn't a whole lot to pick from. She still hated clothes shopping, and well, she didn't like to waste money on clothes.

Grabbing a skirt and a shirt that helped to emphasize the curves she'd finally been able to fill, she wriggled into her clothes and then ran a brush through her hair, trying to dry it out without using a hairdryer. Her cheeks were already a horrible shade of red from rushing, and they were going to look like a strawberry if she used the hairdryer.

Just as she finished with the brush, she didn't exactly have much choice left as there was a knock at the door.

Her heart raced, and she was filled with excitement.

She ran to the door and flung it open. Ink was there, in a leather cut, his hair wet from a shower.

She didn't get the chance to say anything as he picked her up in his arms and kicked the door closed behind him, reaching out to flick the lock. She wrapped her arms around his neck, holding him close as he carried her down the short hallway to her sofa. He didn't press her to the sofa, but sat down, allowing her to straddle his waist.

His hands went to her thighs, gripping her flesh as she rubbed herself against him. He moved to her ass, holding her tight, and she moaned against his lips, never wanting him to stop.

"You are driving me crazy," he said, breaking from the kiss and trailing his lips down to her neck, sucking on her pulse.

Her nipples felt incredibly hard.

"I want you to be crazy for me. Please, Ink, don't stop. I want this. I want you. I want you so much."

The hands on her ass moved up, and she pulled away as he slowly caressed up until they were beneath her tits. She waited for more, and as his thumb stroked the curve of her breast, she couldn't help but gasp. He knew what he was doing.

The smirk on his lips grated on her nerves, and so to tease him, she did no more than lift the shirt up over her head, showing him she'd decided to go without the bra for support.

Straddling his lap, partially naked, she stared into his eyes, which had heated as he stared at her.

"Darcy?"

"Ink, I know what I want, and what I want is you." She cupped his face, kissing him. Dropping her hands from him, she held his and placed them over her tits. No one had ever touched her like this, nor looked at her as if she was the last meal and he really wanted to take a bite. She arched her back, thrusting her chest out, and she was rewarded as Ink sucked on one breast before sliding his tongue between the valley and taking the other into his mouth. He used his teeth, biting down, and she closed her eyes as the pain and pleasure mingled together.

"You've got a body that was made to take cock, Darcy. To take my cock." He lifted her up, and she had no choice but to wrap her arms and legs around him as he carried her through to his bedroom.

He pressed her down to the bed, and within a matter of seconds, he had her skirt off. Her heart was pounding, but she wasn't nervous. With Ink she felt anything but.

Getting to her feet, she helped him out of the jacket and then started to attack his clothes. Ink didn't help her as he pressed her back to the bed, and she couldn't fight him, not as he had her thighs spread open, and the look on his face startled her. This went beyond hunger. He looked obsessed and half-crazy. She loved it.

He gripped her thighs hard, and she didn't mind at all. She wanted to bear the marks of his touch, to look at them and remember this moment.

She had spent so long dreaming about what it would be like to have Ink finally look at her like a woman, like someone he could be with, and to finally have it right now was a dream come true.

He kissed her thigh, and she sank her teeth into her lip, trying to contain her cries of pleasure.

He knew what he was doing, and it was driving her crazy. When he changed legs, she couldn't hold back and gasped. Next, he pressed a kiss to her mound, and as he spread the lips of her sex open, she thought she was going to lose her mind in pleasure.

Staring down at him, she waited as he held her open with his thumbs and his tongue slid down her slit, teasing past her clit, to go to her entrance, circling to go back up. He sucked her clit into his mouth, and this time, she released her cries of pleasure, the sound echoing off the walls. Collapsing back to the bed, she stared up at the ceiling as he ravished her pussy, drawing her closer to orgasm with each lick and suck until she couldn't think or focus on anything but the pleasure of his tongue.

Over and over, he created this dance on her body, and she loved it. It was so much better than anything she had ever imagined, and when she came, she did so, screaming his name.

Everything to Darcy felt right, it felt good, and there was nothing else she wanted in her life but his mouth on her. He pressed a kiss to her clit before moving up her body. She saw the evidence of her arousal coating his lips.

"That was amazing," she said, panting.

"Do you want me to stop? I want you to enjoy this."

"I don't you want you to stop. I've been waiting for this for so long. Please, don't make me wait any longer."

She was nervous and her heart pounded against her chest, but as he placed his cock against her core, she knew without a shadow of a doubt this was meant to be. There was no one else she could have ever wanted to be her first. Only Ink.

Ink had been her first and only crush. Before him, there hadn't been anyone else, and she'd not wanted to give only part of herself.

Some people may think it was unhealthy of her to have this love for Ink, for a man older than she was, even if not quite old enough to be her father. She had seen the pain inside him, and knew given the chance, she could make him happy again.

They both could be happy.

With his gaze on hers, she waited, knowing it was coming, and as he slammed inside her, tearing through her virginity, she knew there could have never been anyone she would have gladly given her body to.

Ink was her soulmate. He was the reason she kept on fighting so she could see him one last time. To let him know that she loved him and always would.

She cried out as he took her. The pain was a quick shock to her body, but she'd experienced a lot of pain in her life already, and this would lead to pleasure. This was about love.

She'd endured all of her pain for the chance to be here in this moment, to love Ink as he needed to be loved. He took hold of her hands, locking their fingers together, and she wrapped her legs around him.

"You do realize, there's no fucking way I'm letting you go, not ever."

She smiled. "I don't have a problem with that, Ink. You're never getting rid of me."

He pulled out of her and thrust back inside, making her cry out for more. He claimed her lips, and she relished every touch, every gasp as he took her. She wanted to belong to him, and there was no way she was ever going to let him go.

Ink now belonged to her as well, and she didn't want to ever let go.

****

Ink held her close to him. Her body was a perfect canvas, not a single piece of ink on her skin. Pale, beautiful, and now she belonged to him. The feel of her tight heat wrapped around him was sheer perfection, and he didn't want her to go, not ever.

"How do you feel?" he asked.

He'd cleaned her up after, and now they were lying peacefully together. He loved seeing her smile, especially the glow to her skin that he knew he'd been responsible for putting there.

"I feel different. More alive if that's even

possible." She sighed. "How was it for you? Was it awful?"

"Nothing with you could ever be awful." He kissed her head. "Are you sore?"

"No. I feel amazing." She curled up beside him, her hand on his face, drawing him close. "I meant every word I said last night to you."

"I know." He took her hand, pressing a kiss to her inner wrist. "There's something I want to tell you." He locked their fingers together much like he had while he was making love to her. "I love you too."

"You don't have to say that if you don't mean it. I'm a big girl. I know I've scared you."

"It's not possible for you to scare me, Darcy. I'm going to do everything I can to make up for leaving you."

She smiled. "I'm really glad you did, Ink. I don't want you to feel remorse for leaving."

"What do you mean?"

"I was sick. I was really sick, and it was a bad few years. I don't want you to have any memory of that, not even a little bit." She kissed his lips and pushed him to the bed. "I want you to think of me as healthy." She bent down, deepening the kiss, and he gripped the back of her head, moaning as she pressed her body against him. She didn't linger too long though as she trailed her mouth down his body. She sucked on his neck. "When you think of me, I want you to always remember me like this. In control, ready for anything."

She stopped at his nipples, sucking each one in turn, nipping at his flesh. He watched her go, seeing if she would go all the way, and as she kissed down his stomach, heading toward his cock, he knew she would.

"Darcy, you don't have to do this."

"I want to, Ink. I want to do everything with you." She gripped his cock. Her tongue teased the head, and he groaned as she licked down the length of him. Just one touch from Darcy, and he was ready to take her again, to be everything she ever wanted. "Am I doing it right?"

"You don't need to use your teeth. Gentle strokes."

She took his cock into her mouth and he watched her take him, her mouth and hand working together to take as much of him as physically possible. She moaned around his length, and he closed his eyes as the vibration traveled up, and it made him ache to spill his cum into her mouth.

Up and down, she bobbed her head, and he stroked her hair, gripping the back of her head, letting her know what he liked and what he wanted. She took him deeply, and as he hit the back of her throat, he growled.

Over and over, she drove him close to the edge, and it took all of his control not to spill into her mouth.

"I'm close, Darcy. Fuck, baby, stop. I don't want to come in your mouth."

She continued to run her hand up and down his length as she stopped sucking on him. "Why? Don't you like my mouth?"

"I fucking love it."

She went back to sucking him, and he couldn't control himself anymore. He spilled his cum into her mouth, growling as he did so. The orgasm took him completely by surprise, and she swallowed, milking him of all of his cum, and he gave it to her, willingly, without care.

When it was over, he pulled her up so she was lying over his body. Cupping her cheek, he kissed her lips, not caring that he tasted himself on her tongue. In fact, it made him even more aroused to know she still had him.

"I'm not lying to you, Darcy. I fucking love you, and I'm not going to leave. You've got me now, forever."

"Do you think that's supposed to scare me?" She traced a finger across his chest. "I've loved you, Ink, for a long time. This with you, it's what I've always wanted, and I don't want to give it up."

He stroked a curl back from her face, and he thought about her parents, about her apartment. Gritting his teeth, he didn't want to start this relationship with lies.

Lies had a way of catching up with people and ruining happiness, which was not what he wanted to happen here.

"I've got something to tell you," he said.

"What is it?"

"I wasn't entirely honest with you about this apartment or the job."

She pulled away with a frown.

"Blaine and Emily came to me."

"My parents?"

"Yes. They knew you were unhappy and wanted your own space, and they worked to get it through, to make it happen."

"They organized this place?"

"They paid for it, and they helped you get a job as well."

She pulled away from him, but he refused to let her go. "Wow," she said. "I had no idea. Why didn't they tell me all this? Why give it to you?"

"I guess they figured you'd work out they were meddling."

"Does this mean I have people following me?"

"No. I've always been here to protect you, Darcy.

It's not a job to me. I love spending time with you, and I'm not lying to you."

"Were you ever going to tell me the truth?"

"One day, maybe."

"Why now?" she asked.

"Because, I don't want to go another moment without having you in my life. I love you, Darcy, and I won't have any more secrets between us"

She touched his chest, stroking over a pattern of one of his tribal inks.

"What's going on in that crazy head of yours? Are you mad at me?"

"Yes, I'm a little mad, but not at you. At my parents. But no at the same time because it means my parents actually care and were paying attention when I thought they weren't. I don't know. We've got to tell them about us."

"I know."

"I don't want to hide it from them. I mean, I totally will if you want to as well."

"I don't want to hide you, Darcy, and I never will. I'm not ashamed to love you."

"Good, so, erm, how do you think we should do this?"

Chapter Thirteen

"You have totally had sex," Tabitha said, finding Darcy in the library around the science section.

Darcy watched her little friend as she threw her school bag to the ground and grabbed her, turning her head this way and that.

"It's not, like, a beacon or anything. How do you know anyway?"

"Please, you and Ink alone in the woods. You, my dear friend, have not seen the way that guy looks at you. I have. I've watched him, and he's smitten with you." Tabitha stood with her arms on her hips as if she was all great and knowing.

"Could you keep your voice down?"

"Why? No one is here."

"This is kind of personal and private."

"I know. It's why I came here. I also heard some gossip."

"Gossip, what gossip?" she asked.

"You know, you having to invite your parents over for dinner, where it's just your parents, you, and Ink."

Darcy closed her eyes, holding the book to her chest, hoping she didn't lose it. "That was supposed to be private."

"Oops, I guess everyone knows."

"I wanted to talk to my parents first about all of this."

"You will," Tabitha said. "I'm just really nosey. So, how was it?"

"I don't think I should be talking about it with you."

"Please, I'm your BFF. If you can't talk to me, who can you talk to about it?"

"You'll tell Simon, and I don't want him knowing. You're both kids anyway."

"How rude of you to say such a thing. Yes, I will tell Simon, but he won't tell anyone else."

"Still not happening." Darcy put the book on the shelf and went to her trolley, and worked her way up and down the aisles while Tabitha kept trying to nag her to admit what happened.

"You really are pushy, aren't you?"

Tabitha shrugged. "I don't know any other way to be. It's in my blood."

Rolling her eyes, she finished emptying the trolley before turning to Tabitha. "Shouldn't you be in school?"

"Yep, and it's break. I pretty much headed over here the moment the bell hit. Come on, tell me. Are you and Ink going to be a couple?"

Darcy stared at her friend. "I've known you a long time."

"Since birth I believe," Tabitha said.

"You've got a bet with your friends, which is why you're here?"

"I don't have any such thing."

"And when you lie to me, you don't look at me, so I'm guessing you've got money on me and Ink being together and hooking up." Darcy was all too aware of the main Skulls' kids making bets on members of the club. She had done it herself as well a couple of times, but she had always sucked at the outcome and had stopped.

"Look, I'm just wondering if you could help a girl out."

"What are the bets?" Darcy asked.

"Seriously?"

"Yes. You're betting on me. You want to win—I want to know what the hell is going on." She folded her arms and refused to budge.

Tabitha groaned. "Fine. Miles thinks you've got stalker tendencies, so Ink will get a restraining order. If you ask me, he really didn't put a lot of thought into it."

"Next," Darcy asked. She wasn't a stalker, nowhere near, not even when she was a kid and Ink was around. Sure, she liked to look at him, but that's because he was handsome. Age had only made him even more attractive.

"Anthony thinks you two are going to hook up, but he has his doubts about how long for. Daisy, she thinks it's a flash in the pan thing, and I think it's real. I think you and Ink are meant to be together forever."

"Why doesn't Anthony think we'll last?"

Tabitha pressed her lips together, going silent.

"Come on, Tab, spit it out."

"You don't want to know."

"I do."

"Okay, he thinks you're doomed because Ink left before your treatment got really bad. He thinks that there's a risk of it coming back, and Ink will leave you again."

Darcy felt like she'd been hit in the face. "Oh."

"He's a guy. What do guys know? They don't even know how to change their underwear," Tabitha said.

Darcy grabbed a chair and sat down.

"Don't do this, Darcy. Please. They don't know what they're talking about."

"You don't think he's got a point?"

"I think Anthony is a miserable asshole. He carries a whole load of issues in that head of his. Come on, don't listen to him. You and I both know why he didn't stick around, and it had nothing to do with you."

Darcy stared at her friend, feeling tears come to

her eyes. "But there is a risk, Tab. You know it. I know it. Everyone we know knows there is always a risk of it coming back."

"And if it does, you'll keep on fighting. That's who you are, and you love Ink. He loves you. I don't think you should worry about what Anthony says. You know he's morbid and totally into his own sense of importance."

Darcy smiled, wiping away the tears that had spilled. "It's fine. It's something I've thought about a few times actually. Not just because we're together."

"You are *together*."

"Yes. We're together. I don't know how long for."

"Don't act like that. I know you, and I know Ink. There's no way he's going to let you go, and there's no way you're going to let him go. You love him, and he loves you."

Darcy smiled. "He did tell me he loved me."

"See, that's a big step."

"You're right. I shouldn't be sad right now. I'm happy. I've just got to tell my family, and it will be fine."

"Wow, you're at that stage already? You're not going to sneak around, have some fun with it?"

"No, I don't want to waste time sneaking around. What has gotten into you today?" Darcy asked.

"Nothing. I hate school. The usual crap. Anyway, I better go. I've got to head back to school before someone realizes I'm not there. Don't forget to take a break."

"Collect your winnings," Darcy said to Tabitha's back.

She watched her friend run out of the library and shook her head. Tabitha was always on the move. It was like she was scared if she stopped, everything around her would as well. Darcy made her way to the main reception, and sure enough, Ink was there, waiting for her.

In the back of her mind, Anthony's words niggled at her. Even as she took Ink's hand, there was a new wave of doubt. She knew why he'd left those years ago, but there was a risk it would come back, and she couldn't help but wonder if he even knew that.

"Was that Tabitha I saw running off?"

"Yeah, she wanted to win a bet."

"What kind of bet?" he asked.

"Oh, you know, the usual. So, are we inviting my parents to my place or yours?" she asked.

"To my place. I think if your father decides to kick my ass, we've got a bit more space."

"Hey, I love my place."

"I love your place too. It's surrounded by you, and knowing you love it, I love it." He pulled her close and kissed her.

No matter her doubts, she would live with them.
****

Ink poured the wine as Emily and Blaine took the seat at his table. One look at Blaine, and he no longer saw a club brother, but his woman's father. It was strange how that had changed for him, and really quickly.

Blaine had every right to hate him.

Darcy was his little girl.

You're in love with her.

You're not doing anything wrong.

"I was surprised to get an invite," Emily said. "Especially as we're the only ones here. Is this a special occasion?"

"You could say that," Darcy said. "Actually, there's something Ink and I want to talk to you about."

Ink paused in opening the wine as Darcy stepped

to the table. "First, I want to say that I know what you guys did. How you rented out my apartment and got me my job. Ink told me."

He kept his gaze on Darcy. She looked absolutely stunning in a dark blue dress and black flats. Part of him wondered if she'd dressed for his funeral, which he could imagine happening.

The club brothers were all protective of their little girls, and he didn't imagine for a second, Blaine being any different.

"I also want to tell you that I'm not mad at you. Ink and I are also dating. Let's eat." Darcy rushed through the last bit and sat down as he brought over the wine.

"Wait a minute, you're not mad?" Emily asked.

"Hold on, seriously, I don't care that you're not mad. Don't for a second think you can rush over this thing with Ink. You two are together?"

"Yes. Ink and I are a couple."

Ink took a seat beside Darcy and forced himself to look Blaine and Emily in the eye. "I love your daughter, and I'm going to do everything in my power to make her happy."

Darcy gave his hand a squeeze, and he didn't think he'd need her support, but clearly, he really did.

"Ink, a word."

"Dad, don't. I mean it. Ink and I love each other, and we want to make this work."

"I also want to talk to the man who thinks he's good enough for my daughter. A word, Ink, or I'm taking Darcy back home with me."

"I'm nineteen years old."

"You're still my daughter, and I will do whatever I have to, to keep you safe."

"You were with Mom when she was younger

than me."

"That's your mom's and my business, not yours, and you're not in the same situation. Ink is a lot older than I was."

"Dad."

Ink gave her leg a squeeze. "It's fine." He kissed her temple, leaving her alone with her mother, while he followed Blaine into the bedroom.

It was unusual for him to follow the other brother into a bedroom, but he was also braced to get hit.

Tensing up, he waited for it, getting ready for when the blow would finally land.

"I can't let her go. I love her, and I'm not going to walk away."

Blaine shut the door. "When I was young, I fucked up big time. I nearly lost Emily and Darcy because I was a prick. A giant, fucking, waste-of-space prick."

Ink knew the story and had heard it told many times.

"I love my little girl. Darcy, no matter how old she gets, will always be my daughter. I want the best for her."

"I know."

"I don't know if you're the best for her, but you're who she loves. I'm not going to come between the two of you."

"Blaine?"

"You will shut the fuck up and listen to me. That girl has been through hell and back. She went through what no child living on this earth should ever have to go through. She also watched you walk away from her once, and I'm not a fool. I know she loved you then, and that love has only grown."

Blaine?"

"I know why you left. Lash told me about it when it happened. I didn't think you had to leave because of that. I get that she put you in an uncomfortable situation, and I thank you for not doing anything about it. You proved to me that you're the perfect gentleman. I need you to clarify for me where you stand now."

"You mean the details of my sister dying of cancer?" he asked.

"Yes. I'm so sorry for your loss and what you suffered. I couldn't imagine losing Darcy. I don't even want to think about it. You need to think long and hard right now, Ink. My daughter could get cancer again. She could be back in that hospital with a similar or worse diagnosis. Emily doesn't want me to meddle. She wants our daughter to have fun, enjoy life, and I want that for her as well. But I know there's a chance at the end of all of this, there could be heartbreak. Before my daughter gets dragged into this too far, you will need to make a choice. One that will benefit the both of you. If you can't handle my daughter getting sick again, you need to leave. You need to turn your back on her, and on the club. Go back to Piston County, and never fucking return. Or you stick it out. You fight with us all even in the worst-case scenario. I don't want your answer now, but that's me putting my cards on the table for you to understand why I'm hesitant to enjoy this."

Blaine left, not giving him a chance to talk or to explain.

Sitting on the edge of the bed, Ink knew Blaine had a right to feel the way he did, and he couldn't help but wonder if Darcy felt the same way.

After he composed himself, he joined Darcy in entertaining their guests. He served up wine while Darcy dealt with the food. No one spoke about her cancer or him walking away like he did last time.

Emily and Blaine loved their daughter, and he knew they were only looking out for her. He couldn't blame them. He'd left because of Darcy, but it had also opened up those feelings he'd kept buried about his sister as well. He wasn't going to run again. Darcy was an adult. A woman who could make her own decisions. He didn't run because of his sister. She was merely an excuse to keep him away. The truth was, Darcy had scared him. She was fifteen, growing up into a beautiful woman, and had cancer. He didn't want to risk rejecting her, or even worse, doing something he would regret, like giving her what she wanted.

By the time they left and Darcy leaned against the door, smiling at him, he just wanted to make love to her.

Stepping up to her, he pressed her against the door.

"That went better than I thought it would."

He slammed his lips down on hers, silencing her, stopping any more talk, and just focusing on the now with her.

He couldn't think of anything happening to her, of never being able to hold or love her. Taking her hands above her head, he kissed down her body, sucking at the pulse in her neck.

Lifting her up in his arms, he carried her through to his bedroom, stripping her out of her dress, quickly. He didn't give her a chance to touch him as he removed his clothes. Pushing her to the bed, she wrapped her legs around him, and he moved between them, rocking as close to her as he could get.

Touching her pussy, he felt how wet she was. He pushed two fingers inside her, stretching her, trying to make her even more ready for him.

Drawing his fingers up to her clit, he stroked her, while kissing her. He didn't want to stop kissing her lips.

He was addicted to them, and they were driving him wild.

Plunging his tongue into her mouth, he heard her moan, and felt how close she was to coming.

Gripping his cock, using her lubrication on his length, he slid inside her, pushing his fingers against her clit to bring her to orgasm.

The moment she did, her cunt tightened around him like a vise, and he groaned, pausing inside her as the pleasure was almost too much.

"I love you, Darcy. So fucking much," he said, between kisses.

"Please, don't leave me," she said. "I love you too."

This made him pause.

Breaking from the kiss, he stared down into her eyes, holding her face. "I'll never leave you. Are you worried I will?"

"No. I love you, and I know you love me."

"I'll never leave. You own me, Darcy. This is not for the short term. This is long. You and me. I won't ever leave you again."

****

"You shouldn't be smoking," Tabitha said, sneaking up on Anthony, who was hiding behind the back of the clubhouse with a cigarette.

"You shouldn't be sneaking out of school, but you still do, and no, I don't tell anyone."

Tabitha smiled. "We've all got our secrets to keep." She locked her fingers together and stretched out her knuckles.

"Are you trying to tell me you know something?" Anthony asked.

"I don't know more than you, you know that."

"It's late, and I'm bored. What is with the cryptic

bullshit?"

She giggled. This was why she liked Anthony. He rarely took any shit, but for the most part he was silent. He got most of his work done by being quiet. Rarely did he have to raise his voice or speak out of turn. She knew his secrets though, just as he knew hers.

"You know they're going down," she said.

Anthony smirked. "And here I thought we were talking about something else."

Ever since they had merged two high schools, they'd been in a war ground with another club. While those schools had remained separate, there hadn't been any kind of war, but drawing them together, and every day they had to watch their back. Their parents didn't know the true extent of the trouble that faced them every day, and she wasn't going to be the one to tell them either.

They were Skulls kids, and they could handle whatever bullshit was thrown their way. She wasn't afraid of anyone, and never would be.

"She's got what is coming to her," Tabitha said.

"When does it go down?"

"Friday night at the game."

The game wasn't the Fort Wills football game but something different. They used it as a code so their parents never knew where they were or what they were doing.

"You think you're ready for that."

"I'm ready to take that bitch down."

Anthony smirked. "Then consider us all there."

Tabitha laughed, leaning against the brick wall, taking a long deep breath. Things were changing in Fort Wills, especially for them, and it was more important than ever to stick together.

Chapter Fourteen

"Tell me again why you're nervous?" Ink asked.

"Because, this is the first time we're going to the clubhouse, and we're, like, together. You know, a couple."

"I know, and I even get it, but why are you nervous?"

"I care what people think. Are they going to hate me for sending you away and then stealing you back?"

"First of all, you didn't steal me away. I came willingly. Second, I love you, and there's nowhere else I'd rather be than with you. Thirdly, I'm going to have to go on the road with the guys tonight."

Darcy sighed. "Again?"

They'd been an official couple now for a month, and in all of that time, Ink had to go on random trips. She knew it was to help people, and she hated feeling selfish because other people really needed him. She was so proud of what he did, but moments like this, when she was alone, she couldn't help but want him all to herself.

"I know, baby. If you want, I can cancel, ask Lash to take someone else."

Then if something was to happen to whoever needed help, she would never forgive herself. "No, no, it's fine. Honestly. You need to go and do what you need to do. I'll be fine. I'm just being silly."

"I don't think you're being silly. I rather like this, how you're missing me all the time."

She wrapped her arms around him. "I worry that you won't come back."

"I told you I'm not leaving you again."

"I don't mean that. I mean if something was to happen, I'd never forgive myself." She cupped his face. "I love you so much."

He kissed her lips, and the passion she felt took her breath away. He had this way of holding her that made her believe the world was a safer place with him in it.

"When I get back, we're going to have a long weekend together. Take some days off from the library."

"Is that an order?" she asked.

"Yes. I want a weekend of you, all of you." He kissed her again and pressed his body against hers. She gripped his arms, wishing they were heading to the bedroom and not out of the apartment. "We better go before I end up ravishing you right here."

"I don't mind a ravishing."

"I know, baby." He kissed her again before he finally released her. "Come on. You're far too tempting for me."

They rode down the elevator, and she watched the numbers change as they got down. When they got out, she moved toward his car, but he caught her wrist.

"No, I want my woman on the back of my bike."

"You want me to ride with you?"

"Yep. We've not done this before, and I also want you to wear this." He pulled a leather jacket from the hold all of the bike, and she was surprised to see it was a leather cut with the words, "Property of Ink" printed on the back.

"Seriously?"

"I want every single guy to know you belong to me."

"Did you give this out to all the girls?" she asked, being coy, knowing the truth.

"Nope. Just you. You'll be the only one wearing my leather cut, and you know that. You just want to hear me say it." He held the jacket open, and her heart beat a little faster. As she slid into the leather, the jacket smelled incredible. Pulling her hair, which had grown in length and was in fact getting quite long, she gave a little turn for Ink to have a look.

"What do you think?"

"I think your ass was made to sit on the back of my bike. You'll be wearing that at the library."

"Please, there's no way you're jealous."

"I've seen the way some of those old guys look at you. I'm not taking my chances."

She burst out laughing, holding him close. "You say the nicest things."

"I say the right things." He pulled out of her arms, straddling his bike. "Get on, baby. I want to take you out for a spin."

She climbed on the back of his bike, wrapping her arms around his waist, pressing her face against his back.

"I forgot one thing."

"Don't make me wear a helmet. Go slow, but please, let me feel the wind in my air." During her three years in the hospital and being on the meds, she craved the outdoors and nature and feeling wind on the back of a motorcycle.

"You got it, but I will be going slow."

She didn't care.

He pulled away from his parking space, and he wasn't too slow. She was still able to tilt her head back and bask in the freedom and love of all that she had found with Ink. This was what their life should have always been about. This was what she'd dreamed with him, and to know it was happening now, it sent a thrill down her spine. She loved it.

"Hold on tight." He made a turn, and she did as he asked, going with the flow of his body as he took the corner. He was in total control, and she trusted him.

Where he moved, she followed him, and it was amazing.

By the time they arrived at the clubhouse, she didn't want it to end. Ink pulled into the parking lot and she climbed off, nearly falling on her ass because her legs were like Jell-O. Ink caught her, and she held onto him, smiling up into his face.

"You're the most beautiful woman I've ever seen," he said.

"Wow, you have a way with words, Ink."

He helped her to stand up, and she frowned as he suddenly went down on one knee, startling her.

"Ink, what are you doing?" she asked.

"I was going to wait until later to do this. I had a whole romantic setting planned, but I've waited a long time already to do this and I don't want to wait anymore." He took hold of her hand, and she watched him pull something out of his pocket.

Past his shoulders, she saw members of The Skulls coming out of the clubhouse, watching them.

"Ink, they can all see this. Are you crazy right now?"

"I'm not crazy. I'm in love with you. I want only you. When I think about my future, the only person I want is you. You're the love of my life. The only person I want to be with. I don't care if they watch this or not, of if Tabitha and the others have a bet. I know what Anthony said about me. I can see the fear in your eyes, and you're worried I'm going to do the same thing again. I promise you, I won't. You're the only person I want, and we've already wasted a year. Life is too fucking short for this."

"But what if—"

"No, I'll be there. In sickness and in health, I'll be there."

"I can't have kids." She didn't know why she was

constantly saying these things as if to talk him out of it.

"I've already spoken to Whizz and Lacey. We can adopt if it's kids we want." He got to his feet, still holding the ring as he held her, cupping her face. "I love you. All of you. Every single part of you. You're the love of my life, and there's no one I'd ever want to be with but you. Stop keep trying to make excuses and just know that you're loved more than anything else in the world." He pressed his lips to hers.

"Yes." She looked up at him. "Yes."

Up until this moment, she'd had her doubts about him, about what they meant to each other but no more. She was going to give this a chance, and to hell with worrying about the future. The future wasn't yet written, and she was going to enjoy her time now, with him.

Ink slid the ring onto her finger, and she threw her arms around his neck, holding him close.

"I love you, baby."

"I love you too."

****

Ink was pouring Darcy some soda when Anthony stepped into the kitchen. He didn't even bother looking over at the younger kid. Out of all of the Skulls children, Anthony was the biggest enigma. He never begged for attention or tried to draw anyone close to him. For the most part he was cold, collected, refusing to give anyone a chance to get to know him. Apart from Daisy.

He'd seen Anthony with Lacey and Whizz's young daughter, and knew there was something going on there, but he didn't exactly know himself.

With a glass in his hand, and a bottle of beer in the other, he looked at Anthony. There was no cockiness about the kid. No blatant lack of respect.

He just stood there, waiting.

"You think I've got a problem with you?" Ink

asked.

"I only got a problem with you if you hurt Darcy."

"You think I'm going to leave like last time."

"No. I don't blame you for leaving. Darcy was too young, and what she did was wrong. I respect you for leaving, but Darcy is still one of us. You hurt her, step out on her, you won't just deal with me, you'll deal with all of us."

He nodded. "Fair enough."

"You're not going to beat the shit out of me? Threaten to get my ass thrown out of the club?"

"Nope," Ink said. "I respect you for sticking up for Darcy. She's one of you, and I know she's always got friends and people to protect her in you. I'd never do anything to hurt her. I love her with all of my heart. I left once to stop from hurting her, but I'm not going to leave now. I won't ever hurt her." He stared Anthony up and down. "I was a lot like you growing up. Tough, didn't give a shit about the world, not really. The difference between us, Anthony, is I didn't have a family who gave a fuck. They didn't care, and because they didn't give a shit, I lost my sister. They wasted too much time spending money on themselves to pay to take my sister to the doctor. I lost her because of their negligence. That shit with Darcy, it opened it all back up again. I'm not going to prove just you wrong. I'm going to prove you all wrong. I'll stick around."

"Make sure you do, Ink. Darcy's one of us, and well, we have a habit of taking care of our own." Anthony turned and left, and Ink watched him go.

Ink stood at the door as Anthony climbed onto a bench. Tabitha and Daisy were listening to music. Miles sat between them, his arms resting over both of their legs, and Anthony was at the back, looking over their shoulder.

Seeing them now, teenagers, the strength and unity within them, he felt so fucking proud to know them. They all came from The Skulls, and each of them were a family. Anthony pushed some of Daisy's hair off her shoulder, and the girl didn't even react.

Now he had to wonder if Anthony's lack of response was because of Daisy. The girl he'd been wanting for a long time didn't even show any affection toward him, at least not in front of them.

"What are you staring at?" Darcy asked, coming into the doorway.

"Just looking at the kids." He frowned. "Gross, that sounds wrong, doesn't it?"

"Totally wrong." She laughed. "I got thirsty."

He handed her the glass of soda he made for her.

"Are you having second thoughts already?" she asked.

"About marrying you? Not even a slither of a doubt." He banded his arm around her, holding her close.

Blaine was keeping a close eye on him, so he knew he had to be careful or risk his future father-in-law's wrath.

"What is it?" Darcy asked.

"I just realized Blaine's going to be my father-in-law, and that shit is weird."

"I love you," she said.

"I love you too." He wrapped his arms around her waist and headed out into the back yard. Lash was manning the grill as he always did.

There were tables laden with lots of food that he knew Angel had been preparing since yesterday.

The young single mom and boy they'd rescued the other day sat in the corner. There was bruising on the woman's face, but she didn't look terrified of them. They were waiting for Michael Granito to come through with a conviction before the other woman moved on.

Sipping at his drink, he wrapped his arm around Darcy's waist, her leather cut still firmly in place.

This was his dream. He didn't even realize this was what he wanted but now knew he would give anything and everything to keep it.

****

"You shouldn't be here, Daisy." Tabitha stopped and turned to face her best friend.

"What, and you should?" Daisy had her arms folded and her brow raised. It was the face Daisy gave everyone who was being naughty.

"Yeah, I should."

"No, you shouldn't. You snuck out, and not that quietly either. There's no way I'm letting you go alone."

"What are you going to do? Glare at everyone?"

"Stop it, Tab. I know you're just trying to piss me off so I'll leave you alone to go and fight your bullshit, but I'm not buying it. I'm not buying this."

"Okay, fine. What is it you want?" Tabitha asked, frustrated.

"For one, you're not going alone," Miles said, joining them, along with Anthony. Simon wasn't too far behind. This wasn't her Simon though. This was Tate and Murphy's son, her nephew.

"You think we're going to let you go into this fight without back up. Not happening. We do everything as a team, you know that."

"This is bullshit," she said.

"And what if that bitch is there with all her crew? You know what they're like," Anthony said. "We all go together, or you don't go, simple as."

"You think you can stop me?" Tabitha asked.

Anthony lifted up his cell phone. "One call to the

cops, and you're not going."

"What, are you going to get them to arrest me? Please, don't fucking bullshit me."

"No, but I can have them arrest the others. How about that? You want to be a snitch, Tabitha? You're the only one else who knows where to meet them. They'll know you called."

"You bastard."

"We're your friends, Tabitha. You can bitch and moan about it all you want, but we're not backing down, nor are we stopping. We're coming with you, even if I do *glare* my way through it."

Tabitha looked at her family, at her friends, and she felt tears come to her eyes, watching them. This was why they would always be the best. They were more than just a club, they were each other's family, no matter what.

"Then I guess we all better get over there before they think I've chickened out."

Daisy smiled and rushed forward, pulling her into a hug. "I love you, Tabitha."

She held her friend, knowing she did, because she also loved Daisy so much. Holding her hand, they all walked together, united, and ready for whatever was about to be thrown their way.

Chapter Fifteen

Three months later

"Darcy, there is no one else I would want in the world but you. You're beautiful, scary, amazing."

"Scary? When did scary get into the wedding vows?" Lash asked, moving toward him.

"Shit. I had these all memorized yesterday. and now I can't fucking remember them. I'm going to ruin this day. I know it."

"You're not going to ruin anything. I promise. I won't let you. That's not what this is about. Take a breath."

"This is the one day that Darcy will remember all of her life. and what is she going to remember? Me, screwing everything up and fucking her over."

Lash laughed. "Now you're talking crazy. Here, drink this."

"What's this?"

"This is a shot of the finest scotch, and you're going to sit down, take a breath, and be calm. Do you want to run away, is that it?"

"What? You think these are nerves because I don't want to be here?" Ink asked, looking toward his club Prez.

"I have to wonder."

"No, I'm not nervous about this. I'm nervous about messing this up. It's Darcy's day. I want her to remember this for all the right reasons," he said. "I love her, and she has a right to love this day."

Lash smiled. "You are worrying unnecessarily. For all you know Darcy is right now freaking out and wanting to run out on you."

"What?" Ink asked.

"You think it's just the guys that have wedding

jitters? Nope. The women do as well. Thankfully, Angel was never like that. She knew she was getting an awesome package."

Ink ran a hand down his face. The scotch hadn't done anything for him.

"The vows are the most important part," Ink said.

"Since when?"

"It's what we say to each other. It's what matters," Ink said. "Since the moment I've asked her to marry me, I've been thinking how best to say all the things I want to say."

Lash sighed, taking a seat opposite him.

"Then you've been doing it wrong," Lash said. "The vows aren't the most important. I can't even remember the shit I said to Angel. You know what counts?"

"What?" He looked toward his Prez and waited for whatever advice he could give.

"It's a mixture of everything," Lash said. "You think when Angel and I are having a hard time, she thinks about her vows, and it's all going to be magically okay?"

"No."

"No, exactly. Vows are just a bunch of words you say to each other. They have no real value. What does have real value? Action. You always being there. When Darcy's got to go to the hospital, you're there. When she calls you, you don't put that shit off. You go to her. When she's afraid in the middle of the night and scared you're doing the wrong thing, you hold her, and you're patient with her, because it's the little things that matter the most. The things that no one else can take away from you. I'm Angel's everything because she is my life."

Ink sat up.

"And if Darcy's yours, then it doesn't matter

what you say today. It matters what you do a year from now, two years, ten, fifteen, twenty. That is what matters," Lash said.

"Holy shit, bro, you should have totally been a poet," Nash said.

"Fuck off. What are you doing here?" Lash asked, getting to his feet.

"The time for running away has gone. Everyone is ready."

Ink got to his feet. He was ready, more than ready. He made his way out of the room, going to the altar. Their family and friends were all in the church. Darcy had wanted a church wedding, and as the music started, he watched his wife appear. The bridesmaids were already in their places, and he couldn't take his eyes off the woman that was going to be his.

Blaine escorted her down the aisle, and as always Blaine last night had given him a warning that if he couldn't commit to Darcy, he had to leave her be.

No one seemed to realize that he was in love with this woman. She was a fighter, beautiful, strong, and everything he'd ever wanted in a woman. All he had to do was wait for her, and he had.

Every second they were together, it was worth it.

Blaine gave her over to him, lifting up her white lace veil.

"Hey," she said, whispering to him.

"You look beautiful."

The priest cleared his throat and began the ceremony. Ink didn't hear a word of it. He didn't care for what the priest had to say.

When it came to his vows, he was ready.

"Darcy, someone wise told me that having a successful marriage is not about the words I say today but about the actions for the rest of my life."

"That's me," Lash said, calling out.

Laughter filled the church, and Darcy chuckled.

"So, I promise you, I'll always be here for you. You don't have to look to anyone else. I will love you for the rest of my life. If you're sad, I'll be there to make you happy. If I made you happy, I'll give you a bat to punish me with."

She laughed.

"Above all, you have me. Heart, body, mind, and soul. Every day is going to be amazing because we're together."

He saw the tears in her eyes. It was her turn.

"Ink, I have had a crush on you for years." She chuckled, as did the crowd. "I would spend my time pretending not to watch you, doing my homework, but I watched you. I thought of this day a million times, and it doesn't even come close to how perfect this is. I will be there for you, Ink. Every day. I will never let a moment go where I can be with you. Life is too short, and I know from now until the rest of my life, the only person I can ever want is you. You are my everything, and I give you my all."

The moment the priest allowed him to kiss the bride, Ink didn't waste a moment. They were now man and wife, and he was in fucking heaven.

Their family and friends went wild, clapping and cheering. Breaking from the kiss, he stared into her eyes, wiping away the tears.

"Did I mess it up?" he asked.

"No. It was perfect. This is all perfect."

"It's not over yet, lovebirds," Lash said.

"Now is the time for the photographs. Don't think for a second you can get away with not getting your photo." He snapped his fingers, and Ink took hold of Darcy's hand, walking her down the aisle, as their family cheered for them.

When they came out of the church, the photographers were already there, waiting for them.

"Are you ready for the rest of our life?" Ink asked.

"With you by my side, I'm ready for anything."

Epilogue

Ten years later

Darcy stood in the waiting room. She had never been so nervous in all of her life. Ink sat on the hospital bed.

"What do you think is taking them so long?" she asked.

"Calm down. It's all fine." Ink grabbed her hand, pulling her in close. She stepped between his spread legs, resting her head against his.

Her heart was racing, and she was so nervous.

Ten years, she'd been cancer free. She still got tested regularly as there was always the risk it would come back, but for ten years she'd been happily married with Ink, her husband.

"What if she changes her mind?" Darcy asked.

"We know she's not going to. She asked us to take her, remember." Ink tucked some hair behind her ear, and Darcy felt tears spring to her eyes. "Please, don't cry. You know I can't handle it when you cry."

She had tried not to cry, but she had so much to be happy about over the past ten years. Her marriage was even better than she thought it would be. Ink was the love of her life, and they had moved out of their apartments and found a small house with a garden. Ink attended all of her doctor appointments without fail. He had never run away again, and now as they stood in the hospital again, they were waiting for something else, or at least someone else.

Just as she was about to lose her mind, the curtain was pulled back, and she stared down at the young woman who had been rescued by The Skulls. She'd been forced into prostitution and had ended up pregnant. The woman was only seventeen, and she wanted a chance at a life for herself.

"Here they are," she said. "Here are your parents and they are going to love you, and take care of you, and be everything you need."

Ink stood behind her, and Darcy took a step closer to the woman. Abby. The woman who had offered her the baby she was carrying.

The tears fell from her eyes as Abby smiled.

"I thought you would change your mind," Darcy said.

"I won't change my mind. I know this is the best thing for her."

"I'm going to call her Abby," Darcy said. "I promise I will take care of her."

"I know. Thank you, so much." Abby held out the little girl, and Darcy reached for her, holding her close. The hospital was aware of the situation, and Darcy wouldn't hurt Abby or the baby if she'd changed her mind. With the little girl in her arms, she felt this overwhelming wave of love and protection.

"I'm going back to my room now," Abby said. "Thank you so much for everything. For giving me my life back and allowing me to have a second chance."

Darcy watched her go and turned to Ink.

"Our little girl," she said.

"The start of our family." Ink wrapped his arms around her, and she saw the love in his eyes. This was their family, their life, and it was just so freaking perfect.

The End

INK

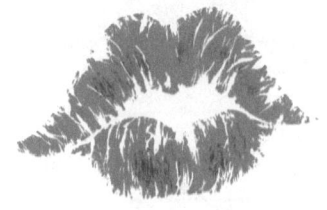

EVERNIGHT PUBLISHING ®

www.evernightpublishing.com